Jacob's Ladder

&

Mercy

Jan Fridegård

Translated, with
an Introduction
and Notes, by
Robert E. Bjork

Jacob's

Tack för himlastegen

Ladder

& *Barmhärtighet*

Mercy

University of Nebraska Press
Lincoln and London

The paper in this book meets
the guidelines for
permanence and durability
of the Committee on
Production Guidelines for
Book Longevity of the
Council on Library Resources.

Publication of this book was aided
by a grant from the
Andrew W. Mellon Foundation.

Library of Congress Cataloging
in Publication Data

Fridegård, Jan, 1897–1968.
Jacob's ladder =
Tack för himlastegen; and,
Mercy = Barmhartighet.

I. Bjork, Robert E., 1949–
II. Fridegård, Jan,
1897–1968. Barmhartighet.
English. III. Title.
IV. Title: Tack för himlastegen.
V. Title: Mercy.
VI. Title: Barmhartighet.
PT9875.F788T313   1985
839.7'372   84-19626
ISBN 0-8032-1969-5

Contents

Acknowledgments

Several people and institutions have generously supported me in my work on *Jacob's Ladder* and *Mercy*. I would like to thank the Department of English at Arizona State University for reducing my teaching load during the fall semester, 1983, so I could complete this project; Nancy Stegall of ASU for providing research assistance on the introductions; Carol King of the Word Processing Center at ASU for expertly typing the manuscripts; and the staffs of Kungliga Biblioteket and Svenskt Visarkiv in Stockholm for helping me track down some obscure words and references. Again, Dr. Carol P. Hartzog of UCLA deserves special credit. She gave the manuscripts the same careful, intelligent, and loving attention she has given to all my work. Professors Torborg Lundell of UCSB and Kristina Söderhjelm-McKnight of the University of California at Berkeley also provided invaluable aid. Both thoroughly scrutinized the books, isolating problems and devising solutions. Finally, I am very grateful to Professor Michael Henry Heim of UCLA and Petter Boutz of Stockholm. Professor Heim pored over the manuscripts, offering numerous suggestions for transforming the Swedish into English, and Mr. Boutz spent many delightful summer hours with me on Agö in the Baltic, helping me focus the translations.

Jacob's Ladder
&
Mercy

Introduction to Jacob's Ladder

The wretchedness of prison life and the prison system's failure to rehabilitate its wards are two of Fridegård's main concerns in *Jacob's Ladder* (*Tack för himlastegen*, 1936). Set almost entirely in Långholmen, Sweden's major penitentiary of the period, the novel realistically depicts prison conditions and intimates what social, religious, and political forces may have caused them. Like the first in the Lars Hård trilogy, this novel thus becomes part of a worldwide social and political movement reflected in nineteenth- and early twentieth-century literature. Many European authors of the period joined voices with social reformers to castigate the penal systems in their respective countries for their inhumanity; those assaults led to significant changes. In Sweden, the Penal Law of 1945 began a period of continuous prison reform, culminating in the establishment of the famous Swedish "special" prisons designed to give inmates specific benefits, such as resocialization or job training.[1]

Prison literature, visceral and dramatic as it tends to be, has fascinated the western world for millennia. The book of Daniel offers an early example of the genre, as does Boethius' *Consolation of Philosophy,* one of the most influential books in the Middle Ages. The

---

1. Ebbe Schön notes in *Jan Fridegård: Proletärdiktaren och folkkulturen* (Stockholm: Wahlström & Widstrand, 1978), p.98, that by the time Fridegård was completing *Jacob's Ladder,* the Swedish prison system had already come under vigorous attack. On "special" prisons, see John R. Snortum, "Sweden's 'Special' Prisons: Correctional Trends and Cultural Traditions," *Criminal Justice and Behavior* 3 (1976): 151–68.

3

genre is particularly well suited to periods of political repression, and so it has produced its highest concentration of masterpieces since the eighteenth century. Writers as diverse as Dumas, Balzac, Hugo, Genet, Stendahl, London, Koestler, Defoe, Byron, Gorky, Andreyev, and Solzhenitsyn have all contributed to the form, helping to codify its essential features. These include the contrast between the debilitating interior of the prison and the elevating beauty of the surroundings, the kind jailor in the midst of cruel guards, the inscriptions on the walls and furniture, the secret prison language tapped out on the bars and walls, and the insanity of the protagonist.[2] All these elements find ample room in prison novels, and *Jacob's Ladder* is no exception, despite its intensely autobiographical character.

Fridegård's awareness of Swedish prisons was raised violently by his own incarceration from July 1919 to March 1920. On completing his active duty in the military, he and a few friends stole some linoleum to buy civilian clothes, earning instead nearly a year of hard labor.[3] Fridegård describes his imprisonment in three works: *A Farmboy's Road to Långholmen* (*En bonddrängs väg till Långholmen*, 1927), *The Wall* (*Muren*, 1934), and *Jacob's Ladder*. The last book, actually, is a mere variation of the second. When his publisher rejected *The Wall*, Fridegård set it aside until he finished *I, Lars Hård* in 1935. He then altered the work slightly, changing the beginning and ending, for example, and developing the benevolent guard to fit his scheme, but the new version remains essentially the same as the old.[4] This reworking of *The Wall* helps account for the differences the reader will soon sense between *Jacob's Ladder* and *I, Lars Hård*.

The Wall was originally intended as the sequel to Fridegård's first novel, *One Night in July* (*En natt i juli*, 1933),[5] which chron-

2. Victor Brombert, *The Romantic Prison: The French Tradition* (Princeton: Princeton University Press, 1978), p.9. Brombert's opening chapter is an excellent analysis of the prison literature genre.
3. Schön, *Jan Fridegård*, p. 94.
4. Erik Gamby, *Jan Fridegård: Introduktion till ett författarskap* (Stockholm: Svenska bokförlaget, 1956), pp. 49–57, 73–80.
5. *One Night in July* is usually considered Fridegård's first novel since *A Farm Boy's Road to Långholmen* was published serially in the anarchist newspaper *Brand*.

icles the development of a *statare* boy, Johan From. At age seventeen, Johan saves his girl friend from being raped. In his rage, however, he accidentally kills the assailant. His life is rather uneventful to that point, and his character lacks the complexity of Lars Hård's. He shows no particular interest in learning or nature, for example, and is more easily motivated than Lars by unreflective, primitive impulse. In the slightly revised version of the book, therefore, some details may not entirely fit the new character. Furthermore, *One Night in July* has a much more brutal and unrelenting atmosphere than does *I, Lars Hård.* Johan bludgeons his victim to death and chokes an old man trying to blackmail him about the crime. The stench of the rapist's decaying flesh, which leads Johan's father to the corpse, seems to permeate the final pages of the novel.

Important as it is, the textual history of *Jacob's Ladder* only partly accounts for its differences from volume one of the trilogy. In *I, Lars Hård,* Lars struggles to find his place in the world, clashing with society and wrestling with himself. In *Jacob's Ladder,* he continues that struggle, embarking on another, more perilous voyage toward personal identity. His voyage—theoretically at least—necessitates a descent into the maelstrom of self as well as of society in order for recovery to begin, a descent into an isolated world where Lars must look inside for strength and purpose. He does not entirely attain this self-knowledge, perhaps because Fridegård does not free him entirely from the Johan From character, but the prison experience is an important event in Lars's life. In fact, in Fridegård's sequel to the Lars Hård trilogy, *Here Is My Hand (Här är min hand,* 1942), which describes Lars's exploits on the road to becoming an author, Lars observes, "You don't learn the most important things in schools . . . but rather in solitude, illness, and perhaps in prison."[6] Similarly in *Jacob's Ladder,* Lars's old shoemaker friend twice talks about the advantages of prison

Fridegård's first book was a small collection of poems entitled *The Black Lute (Den svarta lutan,* 1931).

6. *Här är min hand* (Stockholm: Folket i bilds förlag, 1942), chap. 4. The concluding book in the series, *Lars Hård Moves On (Lars Hård går vidare,* 1951), describes Lars's marriage and ultimate happiness. Though illuminating, these last

life and solitude, asserting at one point that "a little isolation for everyone would save the human race" (p. 79). Like it or not, realize it or not, Lars benefits too. Confined in solitary for four days, racked with fatigue, tormented by voracious rats, Lars is pushed to the brink of insanity. But he manages to hang on, achieving a kind of Byronian or Lovelacean insight: stone walls do not a prison make. He also begins to write poetry and thus unknowingly has an ephemeral vision of what he will eventually become (p. 66). "In its mythic dimension," Victor Brombert aptly states, "carceral imagery implies the presence of a threshold, the possibility of a passage, an initiation."[7] The very title of *Jacob's Ladder*, then, accurately if ironically reflects the degradation Lars must experience to find his inner light,[8] the inner heaven at the end of a ladder leading from one sphere of existence to another.

Although *I, Lars Hård* and *Jacob's Ladder* do differ in tone and are not perfectly coordinated, Fridegård does create strong structural and thematic links between them. The first major link, of course, lies in the character of Lars himself. At the end of volume one, we left him in a particularly foul mood, determined to become the worst among the worst. This boast seemed to represent a lapse into an artificial hardness that Lars was fighting, consciously or unconsciously, throughout the book. At the beginning of volume two, however, he is back to his unguarded, inquisitive self. In one of those reveries that tend to come over Lars whenever work needs to be done, he picks up a piece of rock, examines it, and speculates on its age and history. Some of the old pretension that endeared Lars to us before seems still rooted in his character, to be sure, but now there is also something genuinely probing about Lars's mind. In *Jacob's Ladder* we will no longer find Lars prancing and preening, willy-nilly dropping the names of Schopenhauer, Nietzsche, Emerson, Beethoven, Millet, or Spinoza, trying desperately to believe himself and persuade others that he is

two books differ substantially in tone and quality from the original trilogy and so are not considered integral to it.

7. Brombert, *The Romantic Prison*, p. 6.

8. Artur Lundkvist, "Jan Fridegård," in *Jan Fridegård*, ed. Artur Lundkvist and Lars Forssell (Stockholm: Förlaget frilansen, 1949), p. 15.

more than just "a phonograph."⁹ The Lars we meet in *Jacob's Ladder* is not trying to better anybody. He is merely trying to survive and to understand. As we follow him through the book, we will see more of this genuine quality.

What Fridegård actually gives us in this volume of his trilogy is Lars's progressive assimilation of qualities we most admire in his father. Compassion for and an easy relationship with animals, for example, characterize both men. Lars is the only person in his home area unbitten by a certain angry horse (p. 20); and children and animals go to his father "completely of their own accord" (p. 97). More important, Lars's inherent capacity for human warmth extends itself to his fellows. Although he feigns hardness and callousness at a couple of points in the novel, nonchalantly expressing a perfect narcissistic interest in self, his actions consistently belie his assertions. He takes pity on an unknown, feeble prisoner, telling God to be harder on him as long as He makes it easier for that old man (p. 53). After Lars becomes friends with the same man—the shoemaker, who will soon die—he wishes he could give him two years of his own life (p. 85). This growing interest in others testifies to Lars's emergence from beneath his "hard" exterior.

But there's more to Lars's increasing alignment with his father. He starts recognizing man's insignificance. He does not quite compare man to fly shit, as his father does in reflective moments in *I, Lars Hård,* but he consistently observes the indifference of the heavens to man's plight: the days, the years, the clouds all pass by at the same rate regardless of man's actions on earth. Scolding himself for imagining he has more importance than a piece of rock (p. 21) and realizing the meannesss of his misfortune in the vast scheme of things, he comes to a further realization. Deep within him, he says, "I would have a room where I could go and feel invulnerable" (p. 28). Like his father and the old shoemaker, Lars finds consolation and liberation in his own insignificance. He even

9. Jan Fridegård, *I, Lars Hård,* trans. Robert E. Bjork (Lincoln: University of Nebraska Press, 1983), p.51. Subsequent references to this novel appear in parentheses in the text as *ILH.*

perceives that all the plans he made in prison for a spectacular comeback (p. 97) would never come to pass. Though this perception is doubtless clouded by a degree of self-pity, Lars's partial acceptance of his fate is also a partial rejection of the social norms and expectations underlying his aspirations. It is an important step toward maturity and paves the way for his final journey to self-discovery in the last volume of the trilogy.

Of the number of other connections Fridegård establishes between *I, Lars Hård* and *Jacob's Ladder,* two of the most important are the continuing roles of nature and women. The developments that occur in both themes support the development we see in Lars's character.

Nature almost absents itself from *Jacob's Ladder.* The only glimpses we get of it are in its angry, stormy manifestations at the beginning of the novel after Lars strikes down the guard, and then tranquil, detached snatches of it through the barred windows of the prison. Nature here is always closed to Lars Hård, always beyond his reach. Although at one point he runs praying to the God of the grass and the spruce trees (p. 18), nature does not show him any real mercy (pp. 20, 22, 26). Even the few pitiful plants in the prison yard consistently fail to bloom (pp. 50, 73, 85).

To understand how nature functions in *Jacob's Ladder* we must recall the dark moments in *I, Lars Hård* when Lars could not force his way into it. Twice he found himself shut off from nature when he faced death or the eternal (*ILH*, pp. 21, 80). In *Jacob's Ladder* the fear of both will continue but become less extreme as the shoemaker edges Lars toward viewing death as part of nature. To be one with nature, you must accept death, something Lars will be able to do by the end of the trilogy.

Other dark moments arose from Lars's tendency to project his own feelings onto his surroundings and consequently to project the mercurial nature of society onto nature herself. Lars reacted to misfortune by viewing both society and nature with the same feeling of alienation. After getting the first letter from Hilma Andersson, announcing he was the father of her child, he pondered the cruelty of the human race, concluding that he did not fit in anywhere, "with the high or with the low" (*ILH*, p. 26). When he felt revulsion for the manual labor he was supposed to be doing in the forest, he petulantly flicked away an industrious ant; and when the blue-eyed, upper-class girl finally rejected him in her home district, he found the forest she lived in to be stately, the one he lived in to be base (*ILH*, pp. 46, 85). "All nature," he lamented, "was glad and fawning; I alone sat like an aching tumor in the midst of it" (*ILH*, p. 91). Because Lars is a social being, he unwittingly adopts and is controlled by social norms. These prevent him from having total contact with nature. In *Jacob's Ladder*, the social strictures blocking Lars from nature take palpable form. Prison becomes a symbol for society as a whole, not just its retributive arm. And, appropriately, it almost totally shuts Lars off from what he most wants to reach.

In one major respect, then, nature continues to function as it did in *I, Lars Hård*. But subtle and paradoxical developments occur in *Jacob's Ladder*, showing that Lars may have been still further removed from a true appreciation of nature in the first volume than he is in this one. He once prided himself on knowing the Latin names for plants, easily identifying *geum rivale, intybus,* and *sedum palustre*. He acquired this knowledge, we will recall, because he was jealous of upper-class children and their education (*ILH*, p. 30). By naming plants, animals, philosophers, composers, and artists, Lars was trying to possess them, to become part of them and the society their official names represent, and to make them part of him. Thus the knowledge he displayed in *I, Lars Hård* was pretentious and one more strand in the net that society had thrown around him. In *Jacob's Ladder*, his knowledge becomes more intuitive, less on the surface, more integrated into his personality as he gradually, arduously moves toward a better grasp of self. He mentions no philosophers or artists and uses common names for plants. Although textual history and the character of Johan From may account for this change, two facts militate against such a view: Lars still shows a consistent love for and knowledge of nature, despite the shoemaker's remarks to the contrary; and he can still use Latin in the class struggle. When the prison chaplain is startled by a bedbug crawling out of the Bible, Lars remarks that "a wonderful example of *cimex lectularia* had just slithered across the Sermon on the Mount" (p. 51).

Like his relationship to nature, Lars's relationship to women also both subtly changes and remains the same in *Jacob's Ladder*. Again, Fridegård gives us a relative paucity of evidence to work with. Women almost never appear. We do see some, such as the superintendent's daughter and the women in the Salvation Army newspaper, and Lars ogles them with his customary lust. But Lars has no love affairs in this book. He does, however, have a recurrent wet dream that is one of the symbolic nexuses of the novel, tying together the important themes of society, self, nature, and woman. Since Fridegård put great stock in the enlightening, even prophetic power of dreams,[10] this one bears close scrutiny.

The dream takes place in the churchyard back home, where Lars sees a woman, simultaneously naked and wearing a green veil, standing on a grave beside a cypress tree. Her eyes are a striking blue. She suddenly crouches down and crawls toward Lars like a cat. Though horrified, he rushes at her, wild with desire. Before he can reach her, she sinks into the ground and emerges as a gigantic plant with soft leaves and two blue flowers. He rips off his clothes and clutches the plant to his body, climaxes, then sees the plant wither and drop to the ground.

This dream has at least three important features. First, an acceptance of death is implicit in it since the whole scene takes place in a graveyard. Lars, normally terrified by the prospect of death and the hereafter, is here able to perform the procreative act in the face of both. Second, the scene also takes place in the shadow of the church, which subtly implies Lars's shifting attitude toward organized religion. In *I, Lars Hård* the mere ringing of the church bells stopped Lars cold in the midst of seducing the brown-eyed girl as he felt "heaven open accusingly" above his back (*ILH*, p. 79). Although he will never accept the hypocrisy, pettiness, and cruelty of organized religion, as we will see in the last volume of the trilogy, Lars seems more capable of tolerating the church as

10. Schön, *Jan Fridegård*, p. 207.

a symbol for and expression of man's spirituality. In his waking state, he searches the Bible for consolation after the shoemaker's death (p. 86) even though it had earlier looked paltry and pitiful in comparison with the blue expanse of sky outside his window (p. 52).

The third important feature about Lars's dream is that it conflates nature and woman. What happens here is that Lars internalizes and integrates a simile he first established in *I, Lars Hård* when he encountered one of the three girls on a country road. While talking about coltsfoot flowers, Lars thought: "You upper-class girls, and all women for that matter, you open for the night at the same time the flowers close. You spread your arms and legs out like white petals and wait with closed eyes for the night's silent pollenator. You are night blossoms" (*ILH*, p. 5).[11] In the dream in *Jacob's Ladder*, the simile turns to metaphor. The woman's veil is green, symbolic of nature, and she metamorphoses into a plant that Lars joins, achieving precisely the same pleasure he would have with the woman. What was a forced analogy in the first book becomes a natural identity in the second.

Lars's wet dream, then, which seems at first glance to be a curious but minor detail in the story, allows Lars to begin unconsciously reconciling the conflicting forces within him. He is moving toward the kind of maturity that will enable him to accept with equanimity the fact of his own mortality. As Lars becomes more accepting of death, he also becomes more tolerant of society and religion and more in tune with nature. By extension, he also becomes more in tune with woman. The fact that the resolution Lars experiences occurs in a dream, not reality, naturally implies that he has not yet reached his goal. But Fridegård seems to indicate that Lars will someday find the spiritual and physical peace he has so often sought.

How much peace Lars really wins in *Jacob's Ladder* is, of course, a matter of dispute. The specter of *The Wall* is always in the background, always tempering our assessment of the novel. And the

11. This simile, of course, stems from a highly conventional association of flowers and female sexuality. Lars uses a flower as a poetic euphemism for the hymen or vagina two other times in *I, Lars Hård*. See pp. 15 and 89.

ideas that could most easily allow Lars to achieve a less fragmented view of the world and himself are always articulated by the shoemaker, not by Lars. But even if the book lacks consistency of detail and even if its history makes our job as readers more difficult, the prison experience is clearly necessary for Lars's development. To ensure his chance for growth, he must, as W. B. Yeats does, lie down where all the ladders start. Fridegård makes the beneficial aspects of prison clear through his use of another image. Twice he compares Lars to a seed, and the prison thus becomes a fertile field: Lars would be "put away like a tiny, living seed in one of the cells of the prison's body" (p. 39) or "crammed in the center of a large night-silent clump of stone" (p. 48). Lars's sentence in Långholmen is a kind of gestation period, and though he may not flourish by the end of *Jacob's Ladder*, he will eventually. He will climb out of the foul rag and bone shop of the heart, out of the darkness of his own and society's hell, into a new and promising dawn.

Jacob's Ladder

"Seizure of property, execution, prisons, punishment—they are all unavoidable, that I admit, but they should be administered through just laws in all deference to necessity; nevertheless, I am equally surprised every time I see how cruelly human beings treat other human beings."

LA BRUYÈRE

I, Lars Hård, found a strange rock while shoveling dirt into a wheelbarrow. I put the shovel down immediately and examined the stone more closely. It looked like axe material from the Stone Age, and the grayish-brown color told me it just might be flint.

Between the leafless trees you could barely make out the old manor that had been converted to a work camp where I, since the end of summer, had been held for hard labor. I was working by myself that day and could afford to straighten up a little every once in a while. The guard in charge of me came out from behind the tool shed now and then and set a pair of disdainful black eyes on me, but he had just gone and I didn't have to look out for him for a good while. I sat down on the edge of the wheelbarrow with the piece of rock in my hand.

I was glad to be able to work alone; you could get more than tired of the old men, who always bickered or called each other names or dragged out experiences from their distant pasts. I always thought their stories reeked of snuff and beard just like they did. At night the men lay on their backs in their beds grumpily hiding the tattered magazines or accusing each other of stealing snuff. If most of them hadn't had long, matted beards, you could have mistaken them for a bunch of mean old women. I was thirty years younger than the youngest of them, and they always called me "kid" or "puppy."

Sitting there, I reconstructed the history of the piece of rock. I imagined before me a dense, murmuring spruce forest, a cave, and outside it a heavily built man who had a straggly beard and was wearing animal skins. He sat with the rock in his hand, thinking he could make a good axe out of it. The Stone Age man just might have been called. . . .

Just as I thought up an appropriate name for the man, the guard came out from behind the tool shed. He must have noticed I took a good long rest occasionally, and he was lying in wait for me around the corner. Now he had caught me red-handed.

He came out from behind the little building, and I could do no more than get up before he was on top of me with his black moustache and wicked eyes. I stood turning the piece of rock in my hand as he came, and I could see from his bone-hard look that he was thinking, "Now I'll give it to you, you bastard."

He nailed me fast with that look, and I couldn't throw the rock away, grab my shovel, and start working. If I had done so instead of just standing there with the rock, he would have screamed and yelled at me for sure, but nothing else would have happened. I would have kept shoveling dirt into the wheelbarrow and kept my mouth shut, and when his jaw got tired, he would have gone off and let me be. All he would have said is that he would damn well make sure I stayed awake.

He was shorter than I was, so when he stood in front of me, he directed his coal-like eyes diagonally up into mine. It probably wouldn't have come to anything if he had stopped there and told me off. But he planted his hard, clenched fist under my chin; it wasn't a full blow, but it was enough to rattle my head and jar me back a step.

"I'll teach you, you tall, lazy bastard," the guard said. Maybe it still wouldn't have come to much if I hadn't sensed something new in his look. But I saw he was pleased with himself, satisfied at how strong he was, boorishly happy he had landed one under my chin and knocked me backward. And I saw more than happiness in his expression; I saw contempt for me as an opponent. I moved backward and maybe looked scared. He was merely a guard and had no more thoughts in his head than necessary. You could see that in his look and hear it in his voice.

Wasn't he, like me, frightened of death and eternity? No, the simple soul was strong and worried only about the present. It was extremely comfortable in the squat body, and they would do a long, practical life's work together. That excellent little cog in society's wheel was thinking only about his duty when he hit me under the chin, hissing, "I'll teach you, you tall, lazy bastard."

I wasn't surprised that he wanted to teach me something. Had I been in his place, I would have shown him the piece of rock and asked him to say something about it. Had a Stone Age man perhaps broken it loose to make a tool but had been stopped by death? I, for one, didn't think that unlikely. But he was the guard, and he wanted to teach me to shovel dirt into a wheelbarrow, not stand there like an idiot turning over a piece of rock. It wasn't surprising either that he called me tall and lazy: he was short and industrious.

I guess that's the way it is—a hard laborer has to endure not only a cussing out but also a punch in the jaw from the guards. But isn't it conceivable that I was dazed somehow from my brain rattling when he slugged me? How about defending myself with that? If I had been a free man and had hit someone with a rock, a doctor might have said I had a psychiatric condition from the shaking in my skull. But you don't look for mitigating circumstances in a hard laborer. For him there are only implacable, unyielding legal paragraphs.

I probably knew all that wouldn't be enough to defend me when I came before my judge. No one would listen if I told about a guard with contemptuous, coal-like eyes and a black moustache; about how he had persecuted me for months, derided and threatened me. His voice when he planted his fist under my chin was simultaneously wicked, disdainful, and stupid. If I want to, I can still hear the words he hissed at me when I forgot my misery for a moment and stood with the piece of rock in my fist. "I'll teach you, you tall, lazy bastard."

It wasn't that I was thinking, "Now I'll give it to him." But the latch popped off the door, and since I had hid a year's worth of scorn and hatred behind it, the whole lot rushed forward and something had to give; there was no helping it.

Just as he drew a breath to berate me more, my arm flew out with the piece of rock in my fist. At the same instant I thought that maybe it wasn't the first time the rock had been out on such a mission. If it really was a relic from the Stone Age, that is.

The guard never knew what happened. Everything moving in his head needed time, but this went quickly. He couldn't have imagined I would dare, either. If he had, maybe he would have ducked. I hit him just by the ear, and I saw the blow make a large, fairly deep hole. Blood didn't come out immediately; instead, the hole left by the rock was completely white. The same thing had happened once when I was a little boy and chopped into my wrist with a sickle.

Then, before my eyes, the blood appeared, first in fine drops, then swarming out all at once. I looked at his eyes and they looked back at me, expressing a kind of astonishment as if I had just told an unbelievable story. Simultaneously, he lifted his hands to grab hold of me, but there was no strength in them and they dropped down again. His moustache flared ridiculously, and he showed his teeth as if to laugh. Then he fell.

I didn't look at his face after he fell, just his legs. There were nice blue trousers on them and brown shoes on his feet. One tongue lay outside the shoe top with *Örebro*[1] written on it. Just as I took off toward the gate, one leg moved a little. I ran toward the little gate where the personnel usually walked in and out. I had seen it standing open a few times.

I don't believe that criminals exist before God. At least none incarcerated. As I ran panting toward the gate, I prayed in anguish—God, let the gate be open—without thinking that I had just committed a serious crime. The Bible and catechism God of human justice was at my heels, but I gasped to the god of the grass and spruce trees as I ran toward the gate. It was open.

It was open, but something was moving on the other side of it. Something female. I recognized the superintendent's daughter. I stopped, somehow ashamed. We had seen her many times when we were repairing the road to the gate. She was seventeen and we all looked longingly after her, both me and the old men. When-

1. Örebro, a city located in south-central Sweden, was noted at the time for its shoe manufacturers.

ever she'd pass, we'd look at each other with a grin that meant, "How about that?"

Now she came outside the gate and, although I was in great danger, I was ashamed of running and showing fear while she was looking. The wheelbarrow with the man lying silently beside it couldn't be seen from there. I walked unsteadily and hesitantly toward the gate, the girl coming closer and closer. I tried to look trustworthy, as if I had been sent down to shut the gate or something.

We met right in front of the gate, and for the first time I ventured an anxious glance into her face. I saw immediately that I wouldn't be able to fool her and slip past. She had planted herself in my path and had become one big pale but resolute suspicion. But inside the superintendent's daughter, who wanted to be a heroine and perhaps get into the newspapers, I seemed to see a frightened girl.

"Do you have permission to leave?" she asked, her voice matching her face.

"I was just going to shut the gate," I answered and heard that my voice was rough and uncertain. Meanwhile, it dimly crossed my mind that perhaps she would be like the woman in a foreign story I read once. A prowler came to the woman through her window. She woke up in her elegant nightgown, subdued her fear, and started talking with the prowler. It turned out that he, like me, was an intelligent man who had fallen into misfortune. Later, they got married.

But this girl was another sort. Pale but resolute, she took hold of the iron gate to pull it shut in front of my nose. She had no pity for the thin, gray figure of misfortune who stood before her wanting to get out. I knew that no romantic scene would be played out by the gate. But I had to get out and in whatever way possible.

"Get out of the way," I said angrily, taking a step toward her.

She dropped her facade, gasped with wide-open mouth, squinted with fear at me, and took off toward the superintendent's house. I walked out, shutting the gate after me.

"Daddy, Daddy!" the girl screamed, running on the gravel path.

She probably thought she still had a chance of saving her heroine's glory.

I still refused to run; it went against the grain to run. A hundred meters from the gate, a forest started on the left side of the road, and I walked faster and faster until I reached it. Not until I was hidden among the spruce trees did I start running, and I sensed their fragrance as I ran.

"Daddy!" screamed the girl a long way off.

As I lumbered into the forest, the rust-red, wet ferns hit my shins. It would be a few minutes before any guard came after me. I turned around and looked at my tracks, but my footprints could be seen only where the moss was thick.

After a while I slowed down to a walk. The October day was drawing to a close, and it soon grew dark in the wet forest. It started to rain; the crows flew silently to their night perches; a train whistled in the distance.

I, Lars Hård, good-for-nothing, hard laborer—and today, murderer—walked forward among spruces and junipers that were wet, sharp, and without mercy. I stepped into a swamp and got the regulation shoes full of autumn-cold water.

In a strange forest, I wandered about, unable to look for shelter, unable to let myself be seen. My body, draped with the gray regulation rags, was all I owned, and now they were hunting it to shut it in. It couldn't wander about in the forest; it had to be sought out and punished.

I tried to feel like the monster I must be, but instead I merely felt more deeply afflicted. I had never chosen to do anyone any harm here in the world. Quite the opposite—I had more feeling than most for animals and innocent wretches, and my heart ached for all those who suffered, even if the suffering was not undeserved. But what did that matter, I thought.

There was an angry horse back home once that bit everyone except me. Didn't that prove that somewhere in me there was something good even though men hadn't discovered it? I had plenty of merits other than those recognized and acknowledged.

My hands grew cold and I tried to stick them into my pockets. Then I noticed that I still clenched the piece of rock in my right

20

hand. I looked at the rock carefully, but it showed not a trace of the fight.

I wondered if it had been created and shaped by fate in a primal epoch to spell the guard's death and my eternal misfortune. Oh, hell! We're always so ready to set man in relation to everything else. Who says there's anything remarkable about that particular group anyway? A stone could be as good as a man, both in and of itself and as an independent object.

But if the superintendent's daughter saw the piece of rock in my fist, no wonder she squinted and ran screaming for daddy. To be revenged on her, I thought that when a girl is really scared she screams for daddy, but when she's pretending to be afraid for a man's benefit in private, then she yells for mama.

In the gathering dusk the rain fell, and I roamed across the clearing, keeping an eye out for small ponds lying black and dangerous among the trees, and I took the long way around because of them. The whole time, one trifling matter after another ran around in my head, and I thought about them closely and carefully. I busied myself with nothing but a lot of trivia, although my misery was so great. I think that if I were taken to the block, in my extreme terror I would either count the marks on the block from the previous strokes of the axe or try to see what kind of wood it was made of.

I came to a soft forest road and followed it for a long way. I lost it now and then, and finally I could only follow it by looking at the treetops. One time I tumbled over a stone and fell hard on my head. I swore just as if I were a normal, free, and happy person.

A window shone with a pink glow among the trees, and I thought that people so far out here in the forest probably didn't have electric light. They probably still had to make do with a kerosene lamp. When I stood and saw the black contours of the crofter's cottage stand out against the surrounding darkness, my insides cried out for shelter and warmth. A worn and even dirty kitchen table to sit by, a fire in the stove, pans, a coffee pot. Rough working hands holding the district newspaper and friendly old eyes behind eyeglasses.

The roof of the outbuilding shot out a half-meter, and I ducked under it to protect myself from the rain. It fell without haste, somnolent and monotonous. I was soaked through and trembled with chills. In the barn a cow mooed and sometimes a pig grunted. I thought I might sneak into the barn when the people in the crofter's holding had gone to bed. It would certainly be locked up for the night.

Suddenly a smell of fried pork came from the cottage and I felt how hungry I was. If I had had other clothes, I might have gone in and asked for a little food. Not begged really, but I could have sat down on the sofa and whined a little, then maybe they would have offered me something. Come to think of it, there shouldn't be much danger. Surely people out in the woods didn't know these were prisoner's clothes. There was nothing about them that gave them away. Honest folk could have thick, gray cloth for their clothes, too.

Oh, I knew all right how unwillingly people of the huts offer other people their simple food, but as far as I was concerned, I would have been glad in my soul for a cup of coffee. Yes, in the end I thought that, if I could only have that, everything else would take care of itself. I would be warm, my thoughts would clear, and the way out of my misery would reveal itself.

I sneaked a little closer and tried to look in, but the red-striped curtains fulfilled their duty all too well. I heard a variety of men's and women's voices raised to be heard above the pork sizzling in the pan. I stood outside the window shivering, the rain dripping from the tip of my nose, and I had no choice. The sky above the wet forest was gray-black; it was almost impossible to expect any help from there.

When the steps creaked under the regulation shoes, I almost turned and rushed out into the forest again. But I knocked on the door; it was quiet for a minute and then a mistrustful woman's voice said, "Come in." With dripping nose and quivering heart I stepped in. The one who had said "Come in" was standing by the stove, and by the table sat three men and two younger girls. The cat sat on the floor, looking up longingly at the girls as they ate.

"Good evening," I said as easily as a traveling salesman.

"Evening," answered a couple of the men, and the mother by the stove looked at me, scrutinizing and unafraid since she had menfolk home. It was nice and dark by the door.

"I'm a stranger in this area," I said, "and seem to have lost my way in the dark. I'm on my way home."

But naturally I heard how the lie made my voice thin and false.

"Oh, yes." The older man coughed, peeled a potato, and said it was easy to go wrong when it was as dark as it was tonight. Where did I want to go?

I came out with a place that I knew lay several miles from there.

"Come in," the woman with the pork said, not cordially but because that's what you are supposed to say and maybe because then she could see me better.

I sat down on the rib-backed sofa and the cat came over to me, but turned an uninterested rump in my direction and walked back to the table when it saw I had no food. Now I could be seen a little better in the light from the lamp, and I watched the father and sons exchange meaningful glances. None of them was born to be an actor, but they did their best. A heavily built twenty-year-old quickly ate his fill; he cast a significant look at his father and said unnecessarily loudly, "I'll go out and take care of the horse."

"Yes, go ahead," the father answered, coughing unnecessarily.

The son got up too quickly, searched too nervously for his cap, and closed the door too quietly. I could plainly see how the mother standing by the stove made it clear with nods and glances what kind of visitor I was. They had probably even recognized the regulation clothes, or news of the escape may already have reached into the forest. The son had run to the work camp or to the county sheriff; I was as sure about that as if I had seen him eagerly trotting through the woods. It was probably best to go back out in the rain again.

"Well, this won't get the cows milked," I said, getting up. "I might as well be on my way."

"No, sit down, sit down and warm yourself," the woman by the stove said shrilly and tensely.

"Yes, you probably won't have time to make it home tonight anyway," someone said from the table. Then it got quiet and tense in the room. The one girl gave the cat her bacon rind without taking her eyes off me.

"I'll put the coffee on," continued the shrill voice from the stove.

"Yes, a drop of coffee can't hurt in this nasty weather," said the father of the house, continuing his antiphon with the old woman. But I got up and saw a puddle on the floor from the regulation shoes.

As I stood by the door, everything within me rose up violently against going out in the darkness and rain again. The coarse suit clung cold and wet to my body as I moved. I felt like crying when I say how anxious the family was that I might get away. I hadn't done anything to them; why did they persecute me? At the same time, I was worried that the father or son would try forcibly to stop me. Then several unfortunate things could happen. I was by the door now, and I felt endlessly sorry for myself.

"Wouldn't you like to taste a drop of warm coffee even so?" someone said from behind me.

Then I burst into tears, even though I reached all the way to the ceiling in the cottage. I sobbed heavily, and when I got my voice back again, I said thickly, "You can keep your damn coffee!"

I slammed the door and went out on the steps, followed by the smell of pork. There were no comments from inside. At the side of the stairs stood a bucket with rainwater splashing and tinkling down in it.

The outbuilding was dark when I walked by, and no one was feeding the horse. The cow mooed and the pig grunted in the darkness. With a feeling of envy, I thought about the warmth they had and the hay they lay in. "You have it pretty good, you cows and pigs," I thought, sobbing, swearing, and blowing my nose between my thumb and index finger.

I found the roadway again and followed it. It had deep, water-filled tracks from the wheels that I stumbled into, but I didn't care. I tripped over a dead pine branch and a living one swept across my nose with its sharp pine whisk. From my cap, the rain ran down my back and out the legs of my trousers.

I wasn't afraid of being nabbed that night. No county sheriff with a Coleman lantern could find a gray-clad prisoner in this darkness. And tomorrow lay beyond a rainy, cold, black eternity.

It wasn't far to the edge of the forest. I saw rows of windows in one place and occasional lights. It couldn't be anything but a farm. I figured I had covered several miles in the afternoon before it got dark.

The roadway continued toward the farm and soon flowed into a treelined road. In the darkness, I met someone dragging his feet, someone who said "good evening," someone carrying a pail or a bucket.

"I'll go to a *statare*'s shack," I thought. "Maybe I'll get some coffee there if I tell them my father's a *statare*." Back home the *statare* always stuck together.

Some people came toward me on the road again. I didn't see anyone, but I heard men's voices. The fear building up inside me made me slink hastily behind a tree. The tree wasn't so thick that it could have hidden me if it had been lighter out. But here, not far from the lanterns, it was nearly dark. The men came closer, their feet sloshing in the mud.

"So he's at your place now," said a voice that I guessed was the county sheriff's or the county deputy's.

"You bet," an eager voice responded. "He was sitting on the sofa when I left and Pa isn't the kind who would let him go. We winked at each other, Pa and me, and I knew it was time to go out and feed the horse, ha, ha, ha."

Before I knew it, my body hopped so quickly over a ditch and out into a plowed field that my thoughts couldn't keep up. They stayed behind by the tree as my regulation shoes splashed down in the muddy furrows. Then a thought rushed into my head whispering, "Stand still, you damn fool."

I stood still and heard my shoes slowly work their way down into the mud. The group on the road had stopped too.

"Quiet!" someone said, and everyone listened.

In the distance, a motorboat thumped, "Putt, putt, putt," and my heart tried to keep pace with it. For a few beats they kept up with each other, but then the one went faster and there was a painful skip in my chest. I had to suck the air in with my mouth wide open so my panting couldn't be heard from the road.

"Did you hear anything?" asked the county sheriff's voice.

"Yeah, but it was probably a crow flying off," the crofter boy's young voice reasoned.

"Or a damn dog running away," a gruffer voice guessed.

"Putt, putt, putt," said my heart and the motor barge in the distance.

"My pa and my brother won't let him go," the boy said convincingly, and then the many sloshing feet started up again.

I didn't dare go back to the path; I went straight out into the wide-open, ploughed field instead. The mud stuck on my shoes in huge clumps, my legs slipped here and there, and once I fell on my face in a big ditch. The whole time a cold rain sprinkled steadily down from a black, merciless heaven. One shoe got stuck in the mud and I groped after it for a long time. When I caught hold of it, I had to scrape the mud off my socks with my hands until I could get my foot down in the shoe again. I was near despair, sobbing, praying, and swearing.

I don't remember very well how that night went, but I spent a good part of it shivering under a large, dense spruce tree. The rain couldn't penetrate the branches, but it finally worked its way down the trunk and washed coldly, triumphantly, over my neck. It was impossible to keep warm. To console myself, I thought I would really like to catch pneumonia and go to a hospital. Then I would be treated like a human being until I got better, and someone, perhaps a woman, would feel sorry for me.

Sometimes the previous day rose before me, saying in a hurt tone that I had hit the hard, swarthy guard in the skull with a piece of rock. The rock lay inside the forest somewhere. I tried to regret what I had done, but that didn't work very well. He had hated and tormented me for months and finally he planted one under my chin. He was a man, but I was one too. What's so remarkable about my hitting back?

But from where I sat, I couldn't hope that anyone would see the matter from my point of view. I had hit the guard and should be judged accordingly. He had hit me first, but so what? He was society's chosen servant and I, its enemy. But if he had been a normal, pleasant man, then nothing would have happened. Then at the very most he would have scolded me for a moment because I had been standing and sniffing at a piece of rock. No one but that swarthy Italian type would have punched me.

I wanted to liken Justice to an old neighbor woman we had back home. She had two sons: one from her first marriage, the other from her husband's. The boys were always punching each other in the nose, and when her boy came and tattled, he got gingerbread cookies and the other got a thrashing. If the stepson complained, she would answer irritatedly, "I don't like tittle-tattles," and would continue washing her dishes, feeling very self-righteous. I wasn't reluctant to liken the old lady to the Justice of society. I was society's stepson, and no one would listen to my complaint.

The whole universe passed through the wet prisoner's skull that endless October night. My capacity for shivering gradually disappeared, and in its place a strange, still sensuality crept into my arms and legs. I was occasionally unconscious, and when I came to again I was in some way identical with the forest or a part of it. Now and then I seemed to see towns and people, and I felt an anxiety like nausea. But it quickly subsided.

The final hours became almost tranquil. In the gray sunrise I heard the crows awaken and test their wings a couple of times, then fly screeching over the countryside in search of a bit of meat for breakfast. Then it stopped raining, the clouds started to rise higher, and a breeze went searching among the branches. It was probably not so far to the fields; a couple of times I heard the partridge's harsh cry: "Sheer-reek, sheer-reek."

When I thought back to the previous night, I could see that just when there was nothing to support me, when sobbing and shivering I staggered through the pitch-black forest where there could be no thought of human help, then something had walked beside me, talking in a scarcely audible voice about a light that would shine a little farther down the road.

As though that voice were all I had in the world, I lifted up and supported myself on it as on a staff. The shivering started again when I roused myself, but that didn't bother me. When at last the rain cloud blew over, it revealed an autumn-cold blue sky. I drank from those blue flecks with an unfamiliar pleasure until the soft clouds tenderly covered them again.

I sat down again, this time on a rock in the middle of a clearing. I found a few frozen lingonberries, which I ate, noticing unmoved that the shivering increased because of them. A rusty piece of saw blade lay beside a stump from the time when the forest had been cleared.

As I sat there, I felt the joy growing inside me. I don't know if it came from the universe or from under the earth, but I became charged with a power I hadn't felt before. I saw, as if in a crystal ball, there was nothing to fear and hide from. The cold no longer gnawed at me; my hunger was gone.

High above prisons, love-beds and graves, the clouds had marched for thousands upon thousands of years on their clear blue path; they had marched there before all the officious insects on the earth had, and they would glide undisturbed even after the strange crawling on the surface of the earth had ceased.

And I understood that all my misfortunes had become insignificant, because I could borrow an infinite yardstick to measure them with. I would continue to bluster, stumble and fall, of course, but deep within me I would have a room where I could go and feel invulnerable.

The sky was entirely clear and a fresh wind was blowing. Laughing, I looked at my awful clothes; they had dried a little on the surface but were heavy and wet next to my body. I got up and left. At a hut I asked a terrified old woman for directions to the work camp.

I, Lars Hård, had always thought of detectives as tall men with bronze faces and iron muscles. These two had potbellies and red cheeks, and one of them resembled the owner of the general store back home in the country. But the power they represented was just as terrifying despite their jovial appearance, and the building, which looked like a gaudily decorated cake, approached inexorably in the October haze. While they opened the door, I looked around. I saw some bushes, a mountain ash with red berries still on it, the ground full of sticky yellow leaves, and among the leafless trees farthest away, a sentry box painted green. A worker came out of it and looked indifferently at us while he buttoned his fly.

"In here," one of the men said in an impatient voice, and I went in. I wanted to be on their good side and not make them angry if I could help it. Inside, there was a long corridor with doors on both sides. One door bore a sign that said "Guard Room." The detectives led me in and positioned themselves on either side of me. A uniformed man sat on a duty-straight chair at a hard, official table.

"Yes, here he is now," puffed one of the men who had come with me.

"Good. Search him," the uniform ordered.

Four experienced hands traveled over my thin body and came up with a pencil, a jackknife with a broken blade, a handkerchief, and some small change. The man by the table noted down the objects very carefully. I could feel pretty sure I'd get everything back again to begin a better life on the day I was deemed worthy to make a new start as a useful or at least not harmful member of society.

"Take off your suspenders."

"Suspenders? Oh, yes," I answered, hearing that my voice was cowardly and obsequious.

"Hand them over. Put him in storage until the inspector gets here."

I held up my trousers with both hands and followed the men to another corridor. There they opened some bars, pushed me in through them, and locked the door behind me. Just outside the door I sighted two uniformed officers by a table.

I stood inside the door, looking around. The cell was dark, but its contours gradually came out more distinctly. It was a large cell; the floor was cement, the walls were bare, and round about stood wooden bunks. On the longer side was a stove, giving off its light through the fire damper. Here and there on the bunks lay oblong bundles—one, two, three, four of them.

"Well," one of the bundles said in a rugged bass voice, "how long you thinking of standing there by the door gaping? Come in and make yourself at home. I don't give a damn who you are."

A pair of them sat up, yawning.

"Been here twenty-four hours now," the schnapps bass continued, "and during that time there must have been a dozen devils pushed in chattering about their stories and then taken away for questioning. They bawled and confessed, of course, since no one's come back again. Confessing is the stupidest thing you can do."

"They'll probably squeeze something out of you too," one of the others said in a squeaky voice.

"Out of me? Oh, no, pal. Besides, I have nothing to confess. They've taken me in so they can freight me off to the alcoholics' colony. It'll be the third time I've been there."

The fattest bundle got up and asked in a voice that showed its owner had seen better days, "Have you been to the alcoholics' colony before, sir?"

"'Sir, sir,' do you think I'm full of lice? You well-bred or something? Sounds like it."

"Well-bred? No. But I'm no laborer if that's what you mean, sir."

"To hell with 'sir,'" I said. "What are you here for? An embezzler, no doubt."

The fat one sighed.

"No, but my wife and relatives have arranged for me to go to the alcoholics' colony. That's why I asked. Sure, I did spend all my money, and hers too, on liquor, but what business is that of the relatives?"

He looked around at each of the others in turn and asked again, "What the hell did it have to do with them?"

The bass let go a gruff laugh.

"Maybe we'll be buddies. It'll be fun to see how you handle yourself with the work out here. What do you look like anyway? Hey, pretty boy out there! Turn on the light!" he yelled toward the barred doors.

There was a flash of buttons outside the door.

"You be quiet, Vretholm," a voice said.

"Like hell I will. We have a right to some light in here."

No one answered, but a moment later there was a click and the lights came on.

I sat down on a bench in front of the four men and stared at them. They glared back a moment without saying anything. The bass voice's owner, Vretholm, was a rough character with slush-blue eyes and a protruding lower lip. It seemed specially designed for steadying a schnapps glass.

The well-bred man was so broad in the beam his vest wouldn't button. He had short, bushy hair and a stubby moustache. At regular intervals he snorted, flapping his upper lip to the sides like a horse. His eyes flitted uneasily in all directions.

The two others—a small man with a pale face and one with a powerful build and angular features—sat nearby. The smaller one blinked indifferently and occasionally said a couple of words in a foreign language to his friend. His friend grunted each time and moved his huge jaws. His small blue eyes looked superciliously and scornfully at his surroundings and at the alcoholics.

"As you heard, I have to go to the alcoholics' colony in Venngarn,"[2] said Vretholm, suddenly turning toward me. "The would-be gentleman over there has to go too; what they want with him there I don't know. The little guy there is an Englishman and has a funny name and the other one's a Finn. He's a strong boy, not too timid. 'Ahonen' is his name. Both he and the Englishman are going to be deported."

"Oh, really?"

"That's right. But what about you? What kind of fellow are you?"

"My name's Lars Hård."

"What did they get you for?"

"The charge will be manslaughter, I think."

2. Venngarn is a sixteenth-century palace in Sigtuna, north of Stockholm, that was converted into a facility for treating alcoholism in 1916.

"Manslaughter. Come off it," Vretholm said mistrustfully. "You have to be a man to do that."

But the Finn turned toward me with an interested gleam in his eye. "With a knife?" he asked.

"No, something else happened," I answered, trying to avoid the subject.

"Tell us about it from the beginning," Vretholm urged, moving a little closer. "It might be worth listening to. All the others had done—the ones who chattered away before—was steal something, snatch knicknacks, watches and overcoats. Well, go ahead."

But I wanted to carry my misery within me; I moved farther into a corner and answered, "I don't feel like it."

The Finn, who was still looking at me with interest, nodded his assent. "Well, it's good then you keep quiet," he said. "You Swedes, you just jabber, make the faces, or flap the arms."

"Yes, keep your mouth shut," Vretholm granted, yawning. "You'd probably just lie anyway. They wouldn't let a killer sit here with us; they'd put him in solitary instead. So you're just blustering."

He yawned again, put some snuff in his mouth, and moved to the window with his back to the room. The patch of sky visible through the painted window was a hazy gray, and when the lanterns suddenly lit, you couldn't see it anymore. The Finn and the Englishman spoke a foreign language, and the fat alcoholic sat by himself in a corner, sighing and puckering his upper lip.

The keys clanked and the door opened. An old woman with a big bundle came into the cell. A guard followed her and stood inside the door.

The old woman was big and fat, with a forbidding face. She walked up to a bench and laid the bundle on it without condescending to give the prisoners a glance.

"Hey, look at my old lady," Vretholm said, letting go a coarse, resounding laugh. "Did they get you too this time?"

"I had to bring your best clothes over, you old drunk," the old woman answered. "The police came and said you have to go away for a year again now. Hurry up and change so I can go home."

Vretholm started to change his clothes and the old woman continued berating him the whole time. "When you get out again, you can go wherever you want to. Don't bring your fat red nose home to me anymore," she concluded.

Vretholm stood, trying to put his collar on in front of the painted window. It wasn't a very good mirror. He grimaced and turned this way and that, apparently not caring about the old woman's wrath.

"I'm going to rent the room out to a conscientious, decent man," the old woman added.

"You can go to hell. What kind of a trick is this? You'll have your relief benefits when I'm gone. You don't have to rent anything."

Vretholm let go of the collar and walked up to the old woman. He was completely red in the face and shook his fist in front of her eyes. The guard took a step closer and said, "Take it easy, Vretholm."

"Take it easy? When she's thinking about renting my room out to some guy? You know damn well how that works. Goddamn it! I'll kill both of you when I get out, both you and the guy."

The old woman looked at him curiously but without fear.

"What are you yelling about? Have you ever cared what my life is like? All you do is drink night and day. You never ask about me."

"I'm going to give it to you two when I get out," Vretholm persisted sulkily. When he finished changing his clothes, the old woman packed up his work clothes in the bundle and got ready to leave.

"If I knew you were going to be a man someday, maybe I could forget about renting out the room," she said.

"If you promise that, you've seen me drunk for the last time." Vretholm raised a hand, big as a knapsack, in the air.

"You've said that before, but I'll try to believe you one more time. You'll be welcome back then again in a year. Take care of yourself now over there and good-bye."

The old woman stuck her hand out to Vretholm, who took it and stroked it while he blinked, thrusting his lower lip out even further than before. The old woman coughed, poked her finger in the corner of her eye, and walked to the door with the bundle in her hand.

"Hey, old woman," Vretholm called after her in his trembling schnapps bass.

"Yes, what is it?"

"You don't have a little snuff money for me, do you?"

"They'll let you take some with you?" the old woman asked with a mistrustful side-glance at the guard.

"Yes, of course. And good luck to anyone who wants to take it from me."

The old woman looked in her wallet and slipped him a five crown note.

"Don't drink it up now," she admonished from old habit before the guard let her out.

That night the group grew larger when a boy was pushed into the cell. He was small and poorly dressed. With fearful, crafty rat-eyes, he looked us over and took a couple of hesitant steps into the room.

"What now?" said Vretholm. "Are they picking up kids now too? You're not even fifteen years old, are you?"

"Yes, I am," the boy responded.

"And naturally you've stolen something."

"Nope. I was going to change a hundred crown bill for some old woman at the kiosk, but I ran off with it instead and bought myself a few things. I'm from Hagalund."[3]

"Did you have time to spend it all before you got caught?"

"I hurried and spent about twenty crowns. The cop took the rest back again."

"But then the old bag really didn't need to have you taken in. Not for a couple of lousy ten-crown notes. I'd have forked them over myself if I'd have been there. Old bags never show any mercy."

The gentleman drunkard approached the boy and said in a low voice, "Ask for help from the Care for the Prisoners Society.[4] They'll help you out. But don't tell anyone I said so."

3. Hagalund is a suburb northwest of Stockholm.
4. The "Care for the Prisoners Society" is a philanthropic organization founded to care for newly released prisoners.

He tottered a few uneasy steps across the floor, wagging his upper lip. Then he returned to the boy and whispered, "They call me Mr. Well-Dressed. If they ask what Mr. Well-Dressed said, don't tell them. Keep your lips sealed."

"Oh, really?" the boy answered, looking at him with surprise.

The fat man kept walking around the room looking as if he had been put in there with important secrets. Vretholm eyed him critically and remarked, "You'll be pretty shaky out at Venngarn. You won't be able to take the hard work. There's more to it there than just joggling your paunch in the air playing the gentleman, you can believe that."

The uneasy look returned to the other man's eyes. He sat down on the bunk again.

"Yes, but surely not everyone has to do hard work."

"Everyone. No doubt about it. When the clock strikes six, you hop into your rags, every last one of you, and get a dish of mush. Then you have to yell out a hymn before you set out for the fields. Damn it to hell! It can't be any worse in Siberia!"

"Yes, but what if it's raining?" the other objected.

Vretholm didn't respond. He steadied his elbows on his knees, brooding. His face took on a gloomy expression when he thought about the work camp.

"Skim milk and pasty oatmeal for breakfast instead of cold beer. Doesn't that make your mouth water?" he asked scornfully.

"If it's raining, you must be able to stay inside," the other alcoholic repeated, brandishing his upper lip.

"It would have to be raining pretty damn hard," Vretholm answered crossly. Then everything got completely quiet until another guest arrived.

The last to come in was a middle-aged man in a gray suit. His face expressed great despair, and he wandered rapidly back and forth in the big cell without noticing the collected samples of human misery sitting in a row along the walls watching him.

"It won't do you any good to start training right away," Vretholm finally said. "There won't be any races for a while. Sit down like a normal human being and stop being so damned gloomy."

The new man sat down, rested his head in his hands, and groaned. The Englishman looked indifferently at him, but the Finn cleaved his face in two with a strange, quiet guffaw. Two huge rows of teeth stretched from one ear to the other.

"What kind of a specimen are you?" Vretholm asked. "Whining like some woman. Here's a boy who's probably going up for manslaughter. He could get several years, and he's not sniffling. And here's another one who's only fifteen years old, but he's cocky as hell."

The fifteen-year-old straightened up and looked around. "Yeah, I'll get out sooner or later," he blustered in a hoarse, cracking voice, "and when I do, I'm going to punch the old bag in the jaw for turning me in."

"Yes, you do that," Vretholm said. "Ha, ha, ha. Go ahead and punch her in the jaw. And what about your qualifications?" he said, attacking the newcomer. "We haven't heard them yet."

"They say it's embezzlement, but I swear that—"

"You'll stop swearing here, because if you were innocent and no embezzler, you'd raise your nose in the air and be damned mad. If a man hasn't done anything, he swears, not whines."

"My wife is at home waiting for me and doesn't know anything about it," the new man sobbed. "Now she'll read in the newspaper that I———that I———ooh———!"

"Aah," said Vretholm. "She'll probably get along fine without you. Mine does. Another embezzler will certainly come along to dry her tears with some freshly stolen hundred-crown bills, you'll see."

"Ha, ha, ha," the Finn laughed, drawing up the corners of his mouth so that they almost met at the back of his head.

The gentleman drunkard got up and circled uneasily around the new man, who sat there with his back quivering and his face in his hands. He bent over him and whispered, "Ask for help from the Care for the Prisoners Society. They'll help you. But don't tell anyone I told you. Pretend you knew about it yourself. They'll try to get me any way they can."

He walked a couple of more steps across the floor, followed by the Finn's scornful eyes, and then he whispered again, "If anyone asks you what the nice gentleman in the blue suit said, don't say anything. Not a word."

Meanwhile the man who had just come in was sobbing, hiccupping, and occasionally casting a red, wet look at his unfortunate companions. Vretholm, the Finn, and the Englishman took off their shoes and lay down on their bunks. Since I wanted to seem tough and hard, I did what they did.

Night came, and fewer and fewer cars sloshed by on the wet asphalt outside the painted and barred door and window. Only one light burned in the big cell, and the oblong bundles lay all around on the bunks. One bundle sobbed and sputtered until another raised up on its elbow and snarled, "Shut up. Hey, Swede, shut up!"

My soul was burdened and distressed; the bunk was hard, and I had to turn over constantly. I heard the guards outside the barred door changing shifts.

Suddenly one of the bundles got up and started sneaking from one bunk to the other. My heart started beating harder and I got ready to defend myself if he was after me. When he came closer, I saw it was the fat alcoholic. He sighed, bent over me, and whispered, "I was lying there thinking that, because you're so young, you should ask the Care for the Prisoners Society for help. All the others are sleeping. But don't tell that I told you anything. Just refuse to answer if they ask what Mr. Well-Dressed said."

A horrid stench like rotten fish came from his mouth, and against the chalk-white wall I could see him flapping his upper lip as he got up without waiting for an answer.

The alcoholic stood there a minute sighing, then took off his coat to use as a pillow, and lay back down on the bunk. Vretholm was snoring, and outside the barred door two guards were playing cards. I heard them bidding in low, distinct voices. The autumn rain struck against the window and the morning was infinitely distant.

A wagon stopped outside in the blue-gray dawn. The seven prisoners rose from their beds and looked dismally and quizzically at each other. Only Vretholm knew what it was all about.

"It's probably the paddy wagon. We'll see who it's here for. Probably us teetotalers," he said with equanimity. His future friend got up uneasily, his pale, fat face twitching nervously.

"We're going in the paddy wagon?" he burst out anxiously.

"Did you think a limousine was going to whisk you off to Sobriety Hotel? You've got a good long year ahead of you now," Vretholm said callously.

Two men came into the cell. "Those of you going to Venngarn, time to get ready. Well, well. Is that Vretholm again?"

"That's right. I didn't have the heart to stay away from you any longer," Vretholm parried. "And I bet you've missed me, too."

The fat man wandered around anxiously, tugging on his tie and dusting off his shoes with his handkerchief. He seemed eager to put his departure off as long as possible, and even after Vretholm said good-bye to his cellmates, he dragged himself fussily along the bunks. One of the guards grabbed him by the arm and led him toward the door. He resisted, flapped his upper lip, and said, "This is an outrage. I want to speak with a lawyer. I'm a free citizen, and I haven't done anything wrong."

There was terror in his eyes, and his coat was stretched tight in the back from the officer's grip. Vretholm laughed as the group disappeared through the barred door.

During my first interrogation, I found out that the guard at the camp hadn't died from the blow to the temple; he lay in a hospital and would soon be well again. My relief was immense. When I had some time later to analyze the happiness I felt, I realized it wasn't for the guard's sake I was glad, but for my own. My sentence was reduced by a few years.

Wedged between two officers, I returned to the woods to find the piece of rock. They were very careful, and I had to look at it several times to assure them it was the right one.

At the trial I admitted everything, and when the judge cleverly filled in the remaining gaps on his own, I admitted to what he said too. I saw that it made a very unpleasant impression on the court when I tried to vindicate myself, so I kept quiet about almost all the preliminary history, thinking it best to put the old judges in a good humor. Who knows? Maybe it would soften up those legal paragraphs written in the eighteenth century.

Because I wasn't all that afraid of the men of the court, the newspapers said I had been impudent. If you don't shake when faced with the ancient comedy, you're impudent. I couldn't shake, since I had thought many times before that you can't really tell which side of the barrister the worst scoundrels are on.

However, I was no killer, just violent. The guard would live and would bear the scar I gave him like a medal all his watchdog life.

There was no end to the questioning; the same things were taken up again and again. I realized that a lot of people were living off criminals. My case was so simple that it brilliantly withstood every attempt to complicate it. But I was questioned day after day. The typist typed so much her machine overheated and seemed to glare at me while the chief questioner pondered. The pile of paper grew.

I looked forward with a kind of relief to the day I would be put away like a tiny living seed in one of the cells in the prison's body. The day came at last; the sentence was delivered; I put on my old serge suit for a trip. Flanked by two policemen, off I went from one part of town to another, down a long street, and finally over a little bridge. Just then the autumn sun was shining pale but clear on the leafless trees, on a gray hilltop, on a shore corroded by people, junk iron, and sewers, and on the water full of objects for lessons in sex education.

A toadlike ferry smoked contentedly back and forth between the two parts of town. A white steamboat steered gracefully out from the dock to begin zigzagging among the piers—three cases of gardening supplies disembarked here, two old ladies there. A few men next to the bridge were pulling up a boat for the winter.

Yellow walls with rows of black openings—all set inside a high gray stone wall—emitted an ominous threat. The suffering of numberless people for more than a hundred years hung in the air surrounding the area. Ennobling institutions that the already noble had built to improve the not-so-noble. And in a thick volume, compiled for the people and conditions of a bygone age, you can still find a list of who the not-so-noble are today—the people shut up to be ennobled through hunger, masturbation, ridicule, and squalor. A free and happy clergyman speaks to them occasionally about a stern God.

Some of us with great inner resources, of course, through necessity and loneliness can find we're good company for ourselves, but the average man, with at most three or four trains of thought—what can he do with himself, squashed between silence and stone?

When the policemen turned back, I wasn't with them.

When my guards rang the bell at the prison gate, I looked around. A couple of small boys, tooting like steamboats, were playing in a rain puddle on the hill. The trees were black and leafless, all except a little oak glistening a yellowish-brown in a crevice. On one of the walkways, a woman was pushing a baby carriage. The town was humming in the distance, and at a boatyard riveting machines clattered like machine guns.

Nothing would change just because I would be disappearing for a long time beyond the heavy gate; everything here outside would go on as if nothing had happened. No house would fall down; no woman would tear her hair. The only ones who might remember me, of course, were the old men at the work camp; they would laugh, "ha, ha, ha," and "ho, ho, ho," and say, "He was the one who hit the little black-haired bastard with a rock. You can still see the scar if you look close enough."

The gate closed with a bang behind me and the guard bolted it. He was friends with both my guards, and they exchanged a few friendly words about their wives and kids. "Say hello to them at home," they said to one another. To the left, I saw a house that was connected by a walkway with one of the larger prison buildings.

40

"This way," my guard said brusquely, pointing toward the lower house. Steam and an unpleasant odor struck against us inside, and water was gushing. There were several boxlike partitions in a stall, and in a couple of them there was some snuffling and splashing. I still had some curiosity left from my life as a normal human being; I raised up on my toes and looked over the partition. Instantaneously, I got a violent shove as the guard screamed, "What are you doing? You stay where I put you, goddamnit."

I must be a chess piece, I thought. To have any meaning, I had to stand right here.

But inside the partition, I saw a man sitting in a gray bathtub with water up to his chest and a prison guard beside him. The man's wet beard hung down and his small round eyes stared up at my face above the partition. His beard and eyebrows were light, and he looked like a pig surprised in its pen.

"Take your clothes off," my guard said to me.

"Take my clothes off?"

"Can't you see this is a bathhouse? Haven't you ever had a bath before?"

"You don't have any right to be yelling at me like this," I said, thinking that a man should hold on to a little dignity even if he was in prison.

The prison soldier was a whole head shorter than I was, but he walked up very close to me and, his eyes gleaming up into mine, said in a low, wicked voice, "Listen, you pipsqueak, if you don't shut up and follow orders, you're going to make life hell for yourself. Now get your clothes off!"

Then it dawned on me that they would make it hotter here for me than for the other inmates because I had hit a prison guard in the head with a rock. The guards felt a collegial responsibility to take their revenge in whatever way they could.

The bathtub had a thick ring of dirt around it from an earlier victim. The water was almost cold, and it smelled filthy. After I had washed, another guard came with my new clothes. A jacket and a pair of coarse, patched linen trousers with wooden buttons. Two crisscrossed straps for suspenders. The trousers reached to the middle of my shins and the cap was just right for a child.

"The cap is way too small," I dared tell the guard.

"Can I help it you have such a big head?" he answered contemptuously. "Give me your clothes."

I obeyed silently, and he made a bundle of my suit. "Hey," I thought to the suit, "I wonder what things will be like when we see each other again."

Another uniformed man, with a gray beard and a stripe on his cap, came in after I had put on the strange prison clothes. "What's your name?" he asked gruffly.

"Lars Hård."

"Oh, yes. Put him in number sixteen," he ordered.

The prison corridor was endless, and the yellow cell doors with their rows of black nail heads seemed countless. I looked up and saw two more levels, as rich with cells as the lower one.

The guard unlocked number sixteen, stepped to the side, and said scornfully, "Step in and make yourself at home."

Before he locked the door again on me, he added, "Be a good boy now and don't run in and out too much." Cackling with satisfaction at his words, he walked away down the corridor.

My new apartment was four meters square. Next to one wall stood a piece of furniture that was a table during the day but at night changed into a bed with a table-leaf for a headboard. A smell of sweat and bedbug powder rose from the bedding inside the bedstand.

A three-legged stool stood by the table and three books lay on a little shelf. There was the New Testament, a hymn book, and a thin book called *In Solitary Moments*.[5] Yes, that one was probably a must; things already felt nauseatingly solitary. A white sky sailed past the cell window, which was pretty high on the wall; far away, cell doors were slamming, and I could hear indistinct calls.

The walls were scribbled full of names, insults, and drawings of both sets of sexual parts. Some inmate had written down the numbers from 180 and had crossed one off for each day. The whole list looked like a gigantic centipede on the whitewashed wall. I wondered why the guards hadn't seen it and put a stop to it.

5. *In Solitary Moments: Meditational and Devotional Manual,* by Arvid Salvén, was published by the Royal Swedish Prison Board in two editions in 1916 and 1919.

Under the numbers, the inmate had written, "Free tomorrow—good-bye, you damn gray stone hell."

Another inmate had drawn a man and a woman in an intimate position. Under them he had inscribed a poem:

You may look like this right now
But when my time is through
You sure can bet your asses
It'll be the end of you.

I picked up the smallest third of my library and opened it. The author's name was Salve, and he was a minister. There was plenty of salve in his little creation too.

"Dear friend, events have come to such a pass that you must be here," the book began. Yes, so far he's right; events had come to such a pass before I even had time to feel guilty.

A bedbug crawled out of the book's spine and started its promenade across the open page. It walked hastily across the lines, probably not reading any of those sickeningly sweet words it traversed. It stopped in front of a line, took a few steps first to one and then to the other side, finally made up its mind, and stepped down onto the tabletop. There it renewed its nonchalant stroll in a color compatible with its own. I read the line that had dumbfounded it, and I sneered, even though it was only my first hour in the prison. It read, "Dear friend. You have probably felt, especially in the silence of the night, a gnawing in your—"

Some noise and door-slamming started a long way away. I heard a stern voice incessantly repeating the same words, but it was impossible to understand what it said. It sounded like "Whaterring." Closer and closer. It was at the next cell now. "Whaterring." Was he coming here too?

The lock rattled and the door was jerked open. A guard appeared with an inmate behind him who was wearing better clothes than I was and had combed hair. He was carrying a tin can.

"Want some herring?" asked the guard, glaring indifferently at me.

"Herring?"

"Yes, herring. Don't you know what herring is? If you want some, then get a move on."

The inmate looked at me with a little smile on his face as he offered me a thin, dripping herring. I took it by the tail and was at a loss about what to do. "Don't I get anything with it?"

The guard answered only with a disdainful look, but the inmate smiled again and shook his head. The door was shut; the lock rattled. I heard "Whaterring" again at the next cell.

My mood lightened a little; a little music played in my heart. The inmate had looked benevolently at me and smiled. I hadn't seen a smile since I had to do business with Justitia and her servants.

The herring lay on the table looking rigidly at its new owner. Why were they giving the inmates just one herring apiece? You sure couldn't eat it without potatoes or bread.

I waited an hour, but nothing happened. Then I peeled the skin off the herring and bit into its back. You could force down a piece if you drank some water between each bite.

After a while, the lock rattled again. A small, elderly man in a uniform came in. He had a pointed nose, and the whiskers under it made him look like a rat. Under his arm he was carrying a bundle of barge ropes and rope ends. "Name?" he asked in a thin voice without saying hello.

"Lars Hård."

"First time here?"

"Yes."

"Probably can't make oakum, then."

"No."

The rat threw the bundle of barge ropes on the floor and said, "Well, pick this apart real good. Should be fine as tow."

"All right."

"Better hurry up and not cheat. Like this." He took a rope end and pulled a few filaments out of it. "I'll check every day. I know how much a man has time for. Don't try to fool me. It won't work," the little man said thinly and grumpily. The lock rattled and he was gone.

But there was no end to the suitors. I had barely started to

44

wrestle with one of the tarry filament ends before a new guard came in. His eyes were both stern and sorrowful, his body large, and his moustache hung in a melancholy droop.

"You just get here today?" he asked, and his voice was stern without being wicked or forbidding.

"Yes."

"Sit yourself down. I'm going to clip your mane off," he said taking hair clippers out of his pocket.

"Are you going to cut it short?"

"Oh, yes. In this here barber shop we use the same hair style for all our customers."

I sat down and felt the little mower transforming me into a criminal once and for all. The thick head of hair I was so proud of dropped in clumps on the cell floor.

"How long you in for?" the barber above me asked in a voice like a sorrowful father's.

"Couple of years."

"Oh, my, young fella."

He was silent a moment. When he had finished and blown the hair from the scissors, he said, "We have a boy at home, the old lady and I. He's in school. He's the only one we have, so we thought we could afford to spend a little more on him."

"Uh-huh."

"He's got a good head on his shoulders. But you never know. . . . You see so much misery around."

"Yes."

"Now you try to take it easy here. In three months you can get some mail and borrow some books. It's worse those first three months. You're young; things will probably go good for you again."

"Yes."

"I'll be back soon with a broom for you to sweep up the hair," the guard said as he left. But I felt the quiet melody playing in my heart for the second time. The look he gave me when he left was the look of a father.

I grabbed my cropped skull with both hands and looked around. Winters and summers would come and go, but I would be alone with the same scratches on the wall, the opening where the clouds marched by, the Bible, the hymn book, the book of salve. And my shaved head.

I sat down on the cobbler's bench and tried to find something good in my life, some tiny thing for me to hold onto until I got a little stronger. Then I heard a rattling noise and saw that the wooden slate in front of the door hole was gone and an eye was staring into the cell.

The eye stared severely and impatiently first at me, then at the bundle of rope in the corner. I understood the silent order well; I got up and began plucking in the pile. The eye followed all my movements for a moment; then there was another rattling and the wooden slate was again hanging in place.

At dusk the busy slamming of cell doors started up again far away. It quickly came closer and my door was jerked slightly open. "Take the food," a voice said and went on.

Outside the door a tin tray was set inside the wall with a bowl resting on it. I took the bowl and another guard shut the door again.

The bowl was half full of gruel made of rye flour. It fit in perfectly with its surroundings, by the way. It seemed made for a skinny prisoner in gray rags and cropped head with his bars and tattered Bible.

I poured down the gruel, reading the names, the poems, and the vulgar terms for the sexual parts scratched on the tin bowl, and then the slamming started up all over again. "Shove the bowl out here, number sixteen," the gruff voice ordered, and the door was pulled slightly open.

After a while, the prison was quiet. I heard the stealthy rustle again at the door and could see an eye in the little peephole. It looked totally dead, like a fish eye. What did it want now after the work day was over; what did it expect to see? Weren't meter-thick walls enough? Did you have to be tormented besides, scorched by that horrible organ of sight that could belong to God knows who?

I tried stepping to one side to avoid the rigid stare, but the

46

wood of the door was beveled inside, so the eye had control of the whole cell. I sank down on the three-legged chair and put my hands in front of my face. After I had been sitting there a while, there was another clattering, and the eye vanished.

A clock struck far in the distance. The busy slamming of cell doors started up again. My door was pulled slightly open by someone who walked on without looking in. Immediately afterward, someone else came by to shut the doors. He stuck in his head and asked angrily, "Why aren't your clothes out here? What? Haven't you even taken them off yet?"

"I didn't know that—"

"Don't blab; just get your clothes off. Put them on the chair with the suspenders on top."

There's no denying that my hands were trembling as they fumbled with the wooden buttons. The guard was tapping his foot impatiently. "When the clock strikes, you better be undressed and ready to put the chair out in the hall. You'll arrange your clothes properly with the suspenders on top. Get on with it."

"The lights will be out in five minutes," he added as he locked the door.

I was still standing there in the coarse shirt wondering why clothes couldn't be in your cell overnight. Maybe to keep the inmates from escaping. The wall, after all, was only a meter thick. The suspenders had to be visible to guarantee that the prisoner hadn't kept them to hang himself before morning. That much was clear. There was a big pile of oakum, rope ends, and ropes lying in the corner, but I had to put my crisscrossed straps out so I wouldn't hang myself in the night. Ha, ha, ha!

The prison's dirty sweet smell filled the entire cell. It melded with the silence in such a way that in the end I thought it was the silence itself that smelled. It clung to the coarse sheets as I crawled down between them.

Suddenly the light went out. Noiselessly and with lightning speed, it was sucked away and the darkness rolled into the cell. I groped about for the chamber pot and pulled it up to the bed. Then I readied myself for my first night in prison.

The massive stone building, permeated with hundreds of years of curses, was oppressive and menacing. I looked out into the bottomless darkness and felt a cold sweat breaking out over my whole body. Then I felt like I was alone, crammed in the center of a large night-silent clump of stone like a little white seed. The walls closed in around me more and more; soon I wouldn't be able to breathe.

I tried to reason with myself, but my thoughts quickly charged into each other like a pack of scavenger dogs. In the end I couldn't grasp a single thread; they twisted themselves all into a hopeless tangle. And far at the back of my mind a little mucous-white thought was dancing and hopping. It looked like a month-old human embryo, and it was constantly crying, "You're going insane, you're going insane."

"Oh, no, no, no," I heard my lips anxiously protesting into the darkness. "I'm not going insane, I'm not."

But the terror rose, and I slid out of my bed and around the walls groaning. I pinched my leg fiercely, but the skin was tight, hot, and without the least sensation. I crashed into the bedstand and fell on the bed again. The word *claustrophobia* came to me, but that didn't help.

Then I heard the rats squeaking and chasing each other beneath the floor. The pressure abated; I felt a great relief and the darkness took on a friendly gray color. I was alive, I was a human being, and I was not insane. That made everything else less important.

I crawled down into my bed and grinned with satisfaction as the rats started fighting again beneath the floor. I saw the window now, too. It looked like a piece of gray-checkered cloth against the background of the bars. It was really on the wrong wall, but it was a blessing anyway. I brooded a moment over how my head could be where my feet had just been yet still rest on the pillow. But what did that matter? I was sane, and a couple of years might not be so bad.

I lay there feeling some things crawl across my arms and legs. Then they sped across my face, and I grabbed for them and caught some tiny flat creatures that lay still in my hand but emitted a repulsive odor. I groped for the chamber pot and dropped them into it, almost cheerful after my recent terror. I woke up again and again during the night and took up the chase through my body's hunting preserve.

In the morning, after I had taken in my clothes and put out the chamber pot, I heard a guffaw in the hall and a long-termer's rough voice called out to a friend, "Come over here and take a look. The new bastard in sixteen plucked a pot full of bedbugs during the night."

"Ha, ha, ha," his friend answered.

"What's going on there? Hurry up and empty those," a voice farther away ordered.

Outside the bars God's clear autumn days ambled by one after another. A half hour's walk in the yard every day broke up the gray eternity in the cell.

The yards were triangular, forming a star with the points directed inward. In the center was a glass tower and in it—an armed guard. He rotated his head like an owl, staring mistrustfully at the prisoners. The stone wall was five meters thick, and inside it there was an iron fence with sharp spikes, but the guard stared anxiously at the prisoners one by one. Did he believe in miracles or think that a pair of wings would suddenly sprout from an inmate's gray back and the fortunate owner would flap over the wall?

From throughout the enclosed star came the trudging and shuffling of many shoes as the prisoners walked round and round its three sides.

Suddenly a harsh voice intoned, "Oh silent loneliness, where shall I find a friend; in sorrow like no one knows—"[6] The guard rushed up, shaking both arms at one of the yards and shouting, "Quiet in there, quiet!"

An embarrassed laugh came in response, "All right, damn it—"
"Shut up!"

6. "Oh, silent loneliness" is a popular Swedish folk song written by an anonymous author in the first half of the eighteenth century. A five-stanza lament, the song focuses on lost and unrequited love.

The laugh was heard again, more muffled. During the whole walk, the guard glared furiously at the yard, and a couple of times more I could hear the still-defiant laugh.

Between the iron fence and the stone wall was a meter-wide ring of earth where someone had started growing plants. Big, broad-leaved plants, which weren't blooming among their masses of leaves but stood frozen by the wall, still smelling of bitter hops. A black cat with suspicious yellow eyes walked by between the fence and the wall. I called to it, but it flicked its tail disdainfully and walked on without looking back. "Here, kitty, kitty," the next prisoner called as the cat passed his yard.

A key was put in the lock with a delicate, fumbling noise, completely unlike the loud rattle that the guards made when opening the cell door. A middle-aged man in civilian clothes with a big, peaceful, smooth face came in and shut the door. He looked at me with well-rehearsed friendliness and put out a soft hand. "Good day, I'm the chaplain."

"Oh, yes," I answered, thinking that there certainly should be a chaplain in a prison.

"I've read the protocol about your crime," the chaplain said, his friendliness vanishing. "Those were terrible deeds, my friend. In fact, I haven't been able to stop thinking about them."

"Yes, but when you get to choose your own reading material, no use complaining about what's in it," I responded, thinking, "That'll teach you."

"Hmm," the chaplain answered, starting to pace back and forth the two steps the space allowed. "Hmm. But a merciful God dwells even here in this house of sighs. Everything depends on one's relationship to Him and not on whether you live in a palace or in a hovel."

I knew it was the God of the school and the church he was talking about, and I didn't want to have any kind of relationship at all with him. Scoundrel though I was, I still knew that somewhere there was a good and joyous God and that He was distant from all sighing and chanting. He doesn't help anybody, but whoever can approach Him is welcome. But I couldn't talk about Him with a minister who was employed by the old, hard master.

While I was thinking that, the chaplain picked up the Bible on my shelf and opened it. "Read this, my young friend." But suddenly he dropped the Bible and exclaimed, "Ugh! Do you have bugs in your cell?" A wonderful example of *cimex lectularia* had just slithered across the Sermon on the Mount.

"At home we call them bedbugs," I said. "They're affectionate creatures. They get closest of all to man—inside the shirt. I look like I'm getting the measles."

"We've had a prison boy assigned to fumigate the cells," the chaplain said, "but he doesn't see very well, so maybe a few got away."

"Yes, the ones who took flight to God's word have obviously gotten away," I answered.

"I don't like your talk," the chaplain said. "You're hard and bitter, young friend."

The Bible bug disappeared into one of the openings between the bedboards, and the chaplain carefully took the Bible and opened it. Inside the last page was a poem that one of its previous owners had written. I had read it many times and it went like this:

> Lord, keep an eye on pastors all,
> Especially an eye on me,
> And when a place does empty fall,
> Oh, call me straight, straight up to Thee.
> But let me in my earthly home
> Enjoy the tithes meant for Thy praise
> And as the bishop blessed come
> To Västerås for my last days.[7]

"Hmm," the chaplain said after reading the poem. "You're forbidden to draw or write in books or on the walls. What does this stupid poem mean anyway?"

"I didn't write it. I don't even have a pencil."

7. Västerås is an important Swedish bishopric northwest of Stockholm.

"I'm going to the library and look up who was in here before you."

"Can't I borrow a couple of books from the library?"

"In three months, young man, in three months. Though, of course, you already have the Book of Books, the hymnbook—a real treasure—and my colleague's, the vicar Salve's, excellent little book. Read them with humility in your heart, and you shall derive rich blessings from them."

"It would be nice to know who to start with," I answered. "Who's the best author—God, Wallin,[8] or Salve?"

The chaplain looked at me probingly for a minute and then answered with dignity, "I don't know if you're callous or just naive, but God knows what to do when He comes to speak with a callous human soul. Good-bye. I'll look in on you occasionally."

He unlocked the door, shook his head, and left without offering me his hand as he had done when he came.

One white cloud after another glided past the window. Behind them the sky was blue and endless. The Bible, which lay open on the table, looked very sad and paltry. Compared with the window's light blue motion-picture screen, it had nothing to offer. It had fallen open to two passages by itself, both dealing with adultery. The chapter about the prostitutes Aholah and Aholibah[9] was almost worn out and just as dirty as the story itself.

Under the story about how Joseph steadfastly resisted the wife of Potiphar,[10] someone had written in pencil, "Joseph, the Dumb Jew." Later, when I found a pencil stump in a sack of leather I was going to punch into small bits, I drew Joseph with Potiphar's woman as I imagined they would be in that universally known moment. I made Mrs. Potiphar look beautiful even though I realized that she actually must have been ugly. Otherwise the Jew probably wouldn't have declined so quickly, judging by the capacity of his future offspring. And he most likely didn't leave his cloak

8. Johan Olof Wallin (1779–1839). Poet and archbishop under whose leadership a new hymnbook, including close to 140 of his own poems, was developed for the Swedish church.

9. See Ezekiel 23.

10. See Genesis 39.

behind. That was probably just a mistake in the translation. It might have been a damn good cloak.

There wasn't much for children in the 1819 hymnbook either. There were a few things about the earth, the lilies, and spring that you could read like poems. The others were terrible with their blood-and-tears atmosphere or their church-cold promises of a harp-twanging, palm-waving bliss someplace in the universe. The Savior was represented everywhere by a lamb—a dumb, compliant little animal. "How can you give the impression of a person's greatness by likening him to such an insignificant creature?" I wondered.

On the path in the yard, an old man with one leg shorter than the other staggered in front of me toward the half-hour star. He was stooped over, and his beard hung all the way down to his waist. Maybe he would never again be able to see life outside these walls. Before he disappeared behind the plated door, he turned around and looked at me following a few steps behind him. His eyes were as dull as a pair of tin buttons, and his beard was quivering.

All the next night I lay awake chewing on a prayer: "God, if you exist, please don't let me die here; let me live at least another year, another summer on the outside. And please help the old man I saw today. You can lay it on me a little thicker, just as long as you help him out. Amen."

Two nights a week the cell doors were opened a crack and an invisible minister gave a short sermon. His voice rolled back and forth down the long corridors, making it impossible to understand the words. But it probably didn't matter.

The older prisoners had probably grown accustomed to the strange acoustics because they understood the hymn numbers and could sing along. In a cell next to mine, an inmate sang in a loud, resounding voice, showing that its owner sang with joy and pride.

If I listened carefully, I could hear a low, melancholy humming mixed in with the song. Something told me that it was the old man with one leg shorter than the other who was singing. Maybe he was mumbling out a weak hope of pacifying the stern God standing on the other side of the final door he now faced.

One morning I saw snow on the cell's iron bars, and the sky was a cold green. In the yards, the hoplike plants rose frozen out of the snow, and the guard in the tower was wearing a fur coat.

I jogged quickly round and around in my yard to keep warm, my half-meter-long shoes ploughing through the snow. I heard my fellow inmates in the adjacent yards swearing, blowing on their fingers, and slapping their hands. Bearded, ugly, and freezing, I ran around in my yard, my ears like two flames on the sides of my head. I was bareheaded; the cap was so little it wouldn't stay on.

The guard with the bushy moustache was sitting in the tower, and he looked at me several times. When it was finally my turn to go in, he pulled down the window in the tower and asked sternly, "Don't you have a cap?"

"It's way too little," I answered, pulling my hands up out of the openings where the trouser pockets should be.

The guard motioned for me to keep going. At dusk, the cell door was carefully opened and he came in.

"Bring your little cap here, but fast while the corridor is empty," he said softly. Amazed, I found my cap, and he disappeared with it. In a few minutes he came back with a bigger cap. "Here. Now don't let me catch you without one," he said sternly. "And don't go blabbing to the chaplain or someone that I changed it for you. It's none of their business."

I looked at him, thankful and surprised, and took his hand. He was about fifty years old with a bushy, droopy moustache. He drew his hand away and said in a different voice, "There's nothing to thank me for. We have a boy at home. . . . He'll be grown soon and you never know—It was a good thing this cap fit." He broke off sternly, leaving the cell.

Sundays, full of dry, shapeless longing, lay like agony beyond the six days of work. After the croaking voice in the corridor had said "Amen," the bit of meat and the three potatoes had been swallowed, and as many of the guards as could be spared had received permission to go home, the Sunday afternoon started its painful snail's trek through the cells. Those three books grinned tiresomely with their broken spines and without a single new word to offer. You studied the poems, the names, and the sexual parts on the walls until you couldn't stand them, and the blue or gray mil-lionth part of the universe was always just as blue or gray. The lump in my chest grew suffocating.

A fly living in my cell the whole autumn ate from my food and with its buzzing reminded me of the *statare* kitchen back home; it lay dead on its back in the window now, its legs curled up. Occa-sionally, a bird flew like a flash past the window or a crow's cawing pressed in upon me.

If the stone grave had been solid, I could have cried, howled, and raised hell, but suddenly there was a slow rattling at the door and I sat at someone's mercy. What did they think I was doing? Naturally it was forbidden to work on Sundays. What did he want to see? The eye burned, stared, and vanished, but I didn't hear any steps.

The city[11] sent the noise of clanking metal and distant train sig-nals to me. I had been moved into another cell where there was a punching machine. There was a pedal on it and I was supposed to punch bits out of scrap leather given to me in sacks from the shoemaker's shop. Punches were rumbling in the cells on both sides of me.

"You have to stamp hard and punch the bits out whole," said the ratlike guard when he was teaching me how to use the punch. "Or else. If you're good at it, you'll get a few öre a week for sau-sage and margarine. You earn less with the oakum."

I wasn't happy about the change in work, though the sausage and margarine rang sweetly in my ears. The punch rumbled as it popped out bits of leather and reminded me more than the silent oakum had of prison work. When I sat fiddling with it, I could catch some evidence of life outside the walls—the cry of birds, or the factory whistles. One day when the ground was frozen I heard a pair of prisoner's shoes outside plodding and clomping. The man filling the shoes carried something that rattled in time with his

11. Stockholm.

walk. Suddenly someone called him softly from a cell, "Hey, you."

He stopped and answered still more softly, "Yes, what do you want?"

"Do we get rutabagas or potatoes today?"

"Potatoes."

"Great," the convict answered from the cell opening, and the prisoner with the tin bucket kept plodding across the frozen yard.

A little bundle of leather bits bound together with shoemaker's thread fell at my feet. I didn't pick it up immediately and didn't stop, but kept wandering around the triangle as if nothing had happened. I didn't look at the guard until I had turned the corner. He sat as usual, moving his head round to all the yards, and by the calm expression on his face, I knew he hadn't seen anything unusual. When he turned the back of his head to me, I bent down quickly for the leather bundle and stuffed it inside my shirt.

I didn't know what it meant, but the object had fallen at my feet; it had tumbled into my gray day and made me unbearably curious. The minutes left of my walk in the yard became hours. I longed for that moment when I could take out the leather bundle and examine it in the privacy of my cell.

Meanwhile I tried to figure out where it could have come from. I was walking in number three, so someone in number two or number four must have thrown it. It was probably four; it had fallen in such a way as to make that more likely. I would turn around in my cell door and maybe catch a glimpse of him at a suitable distance as he left his yard.

The first metal door clattered, then the second, then the bolt dropped from mine, followed by the armed guard's nod to me that my turn had come.

Just as I walked into my cell, I looked around. Number four came in through the corridor and changed his walking shoes for a pair of indoor shoes from the shoe rack by the door. He was a big man with white, short-cropped hair and white stubble over the lower half of his face. He looked like hell. But he didn't look at me; he probably didn't dare because of the guard standing by the shoe rack.

When the door was locked and the guard's steps had died away, I took out my treasure and looked at it more closely. I gave a start when I saw inscriptions on the leather bits. Someone had carved words on them with a nail or some other sharp object.

"Unknown friend of misfortune holding this message in your hand," the inscription began. I tore open the bundle to see whose signature was on the last bit. I had time to see a few words: "Let this message pass over the wall from left to right."

The whole time I was standing there with the leather bits in my hand I felt a vague uneasiness, a premonition of ruin. I'd felt that before but never so clearly as now. Danger poured through the air from the door, and even before I looked toward the peephole, I knew that an eye was sitting there, an eye without mercy. The one to whom the coldly glittering organ of sight belonged must have sneaked up to the door. I hadn't heard anything but the distant clattering of metal doors that were still opening one at a time, giving out a gray creature who trudged toward his own crypt in that huge stone misery.

Now a small, quick-thinking man might have had time to throw the leather bits in the sack or out through the window, but I have always been slow when it comes to saving myself. Although I was in prison, in some clumsy way I was honest. That kind of honesty has more than once sent me to my doom.

Naturally I stood there, tall and dumb with the leather bits in my fist, when the door opened and the work officer's rat-sharp face became visible. His small wicked eyes sparkled as he walked up to me. "What are you doing?" he asked with menacing calmness. "Give it here."

I handed him the leather bits and his small yellow hands quivered with eagerness as he took them. "Aha," he said delightedly when he saw the words on them, "You're writing a letter. Oh, you're a fine one, aren't you?"

"I didn't write that," I said.

"No, of course not, ha, ha, ha! You found it, naturally."

"Yes."

"Hee, hee, the same old song. In the leather sack there, of course."

"Yes," I answered again, thinking that it was certainly unnecessary to squeal on the one who threw the bundle. But the rat laughed as if I had said something funny. His eyes glistened and his whiskers spread apart.

"I must tell you that the leather is inspected before it's put in the sacks. You're going to hear about this. You'll see."

He took the leather bits and thread, glanced maliciously at me, and left.

I wasn't all that nervous when a while later I was taken away by an officer. Picking up the leather bundle was no great offense, I thought.

I was taken into a big office where a man dressed in civilian clothes sat behind the desk. I had a feeling that he was the warden. The moment when the officer knocked on the door, he arranged his face in respectful wrinkles.

"Here's number sixteen."

"That's fine. Wait outside the door," the civilian answered.

"Yes, warden." The officer went out and I was left alone with the man of power.

He watched me from some endless distance as if he were far removed from anything connected with sinful and unfortunate human beings. Otherwise he looked fine and good; when he spoke, his voice was calm and disinterested. The leather bundle sat before him on the table.

He began by saying that an attempt at agitation and disruption within the prison was regarded as a particularly great offense. He hoped I hadn't involved myself in anything of the kind before. He also expected I would tell the truth and not hide anything. He had ways both of getting at the truth and of seeing that nothing like this would happen again. Now, what was the meaning of the message on the leather?

He spoke level-headedly the whole time, and to repay him I decided to tell him what happened. I wouldn't say from which side the bundle was thrown because I didn't know for sure. "Someone threw it while I was walking in the yard," I said. "That's all I know. I haven't even read it."

The warden tapped his white hand impatiently. "The officer saw you in your cell with the object in your hand," he said. "I don't think you're stupid; why should you try to lie? It's best for you to admit everything. What kind of a sharp instrument did you use to carve this with?"

"I haven't carved anything and I'm not lying. I don't even know what it says on the leather bits."

"All I know is the facts," the warden said coldly. "We caught you red-handed at one of the most serious violations of prison regulations, and I have to decide the punishment. Since you insolently deny your guilt, I have no reason to lighten the punishment."

"It all happened like I said," I persisted, and I couldn't help sounding impudent.

The warden glanced across the eternity between two human beings and pressed a button on the table. The prison guard came in.

"Have you searched the cell carefully?" the warden asked.

"Yes, sir, warden."

"Well?"

"There was no sharp object there."

"Take him back and arrange for a body search. And tell the head guard to come here," the warden ordered.

An hour after the body search, the work officer came in and grabbed the leather sack. "I'll take this," he said, showing his teeth under his whiskers. "You won't be needing it for a few days."

"How's that?"

"You get to move one floor down. And that serves you goddamn right."

I didn't know what he meant but had a feeling that he was hinting at my impending punishment. I saw furrowed malice in his yellow face. I wouldn't want to be him, I thought, and really felt pretty good in comparison.

"Damn it," I said pretty loud after him.

He spun around in confused, irresolute anger. "What did you say?" he screamed shrilly, but then he calmed down and left.

In the afternoon, two guards came to me where I stood punching apart the leather bits the rat had left me with.

"You can stop that and come with us," they said. "Now you get to rest awhile."

The rat stood in the corridor, and when I passed by between my guards, he said in a low triumphant voice, "Now you're in for it, you bastard."

We went down a stone staircase. The cellar smell grew stronger and stronger, and the walls dripped with moisture. At the far end of the long walkway, one of the guards unlocked a door of iron bars and said, "Step in."

I walked hesitantly in. The cell was of about the same dimensions as the one I had just left. By the far wall stood a wooden bench; otherwise it was empty.

I went nosing around the cell like a calf in a new stall. The prison guards stood there a few moments outside the bars, and as far as I could see, there was undisguised joy in their looks. They talked cheerfully and walked up the steps; a door closed and everything became quiet.

The opening in the barred door that let in the light from the dusk was down near ground level. Some yellow blades of grass and blackened stalks of mugwort swayed stiffly in front of the opening, and one time it was blocked by a cat, sniffing and trying to look down into the cellar.

Darkness closed in quickly in the cell. Sometimes there was a loud rustling in a corner, and I could hear indistinct pattering sounds. Once, muffled screams and howls filtered in through the wall.

Suddenly, a light was turned on in the cellar corridor. It hung far away, so only a ray of light reached me. It fell diagonally on a peculiar object set in the door, a kind of tin trough with one side sticking outside the door. What was that for?

The strange rustling noise continued, but I couldn't figure out where it came from. I also heard weak, animal-like snorting somewhere. A couple of hours passed.

I heard steps on the stairway and could dimly see a prisoner's gray rags in the ray of light. Behind him shone the guard's buttons.

"Dump the mush there," the guard ordered.

"And the milk?" the inmate asked.

"Yes, that too."

A gray mass rolled into the tin trough. Then the milk gushed a thin blue over it, and it all settled in the lowest part of the trough, which was facing me.

"Hello in there, you have a spoon don't you?" the prison guard called through the bars.

"Spoon? No."

"Damned carelessness. There should be a spoon. Feel around on the floor; see if it's fallen down."

I scratched on the floor and soon found a ladlelike wooden object. I held it up in the ray of light and saw that the rats had gnawed off half the scoop. "Can I have a real spoon? The rats have gotten to this one."

"They're probably just as clean around the mouth as you are," the guard answered brutally, and the inmate outside laughed ingratiatingly. Then their steps died away on the staircase and the door was shut again.

I wiped the spoon off on my shirt but the disgusting smell of rat made it impossible to eat with. I finally discovered I could hold my nose with my left hand while shoveling the mush in from the trough with my right. I left more than half the mess behind in the trough's corners and edges.

The whole time, the rustling continued round about me, and there was a funny slithering inside the stone wall. It sounded like the big rats were rocking a loose stone. Something dashed across my foot, and I kicked violently as a shudder passed through my body.

I stretched out on the wooden bunk after shoveling the mess into me; I lay there listening to the many different sounds. I could make out the sound of rats dragging their long naked tails along the floor. Sometimes they came so close that the rank odor struck me in the face; sometimes they slashed at each other, squealing like little pigs.

A big rat stuck its nose out in the stream of light, sniffed the air, and stroked its whiskers. When nothing happened, it let its whole body out of the darkness into the ray of light and investigated it carefully. More rats followed, some half-grown with mighty tails, and some old with chewed-up ears and hairless bodies. They moved fitfully here and there, sniffing and staring with black, motionless, beady eyes.

Suddenly the ray of light disappeared, and I heard the surprised rats scamper in every direction. Darkness rolled into the cell, and I sensed that one of my life's most terrible nights was at hand. Until then, I had tried to believe that I would be removed from the cell of punishment before night fell, that no human being in this day and age would be locked up in a dungeon swarming with rats. You never heard about such things, and they were never in the newspapers.

One shudder after another coursed down my spine, though I tried to persuade myself through dry lips to be courageous and manly. "Rats," I said out loud, laughing disdainfully. "A few rats don't scare me. I've seen worse."

A strong disinfectant smell rose from the wooden bench I was sitting on. I got up, lifted the top, and found it was the lid of a latrine. The rats were running around wildly there too, sometimes bumping into a tin mug, making it give out a muffled sound.

A distant light outside shining through the window suddenly went out and the darkness was total.

I groped my way to the bunk again and lay down, using my arm as a pillow. I couldn't lie there for long before my vertebrae ached and I had to change positions. At first I heard the rats running toward their hole every time I moved, but soon their respect was gone and they took no notice. They scratched, fought, and squeaked a half meter below my face, and their rank smell rose up from the floor through the dimness. I screamed at them and kicked the frame of the bunk, but they carried on their private affairs without interruption.

I lapsed into a kind of trance. While sleeping, I sensed the whole time how tender my vertebrae were. The cell disappeared and I was lying in some tall grass with bluebells and oxeye daisies in it. High above the spikes and panicles of the grasses, I saw the tops of some aspens rustling solemnly, and in rapid flashes they revealed the silver linings of their innumerable leaves.

But in the grass on the other side, which I couldn't see, something dangerous was approaching, creeping from hiding place to hiding place and scaring me. Then the grass and aspens were gone, the ground was frozen and hard, and my vertebrae ached again. . . .

I jumped up with a shooting pain in my left hand; I bumped around in the darkness, colliding into the walls before anything became clear to me. I heard the rustling as the rats rushed to their holes, and then all was quiet.

I groped my way back to the bunk and tried to understand what had happened. My left little finger ached fiercely and felt sticky on the end. A rat must have climbed up and bitten me while I was asleep. Yes, I sensed more than heard two of them plop on the floor when I jumped up.

Far away, a clock started striking. It was the stern prison clock that had measured out the misery of countless inmates for hundreds of years. It beat with short, husky strokes excellently adapted to a prisoner's life. I could count out the time now; maybe I had been asleep a long time. "One, two, three, wonderful, four, thank God, soon morning, five, really, six, seven, no. What now, eight, nine, ten, merciful God, no more!"

The rat dance was soon in full swing again; I pulled my feet up and listened carefully in case any tried clambering up to me. Suddenly the tin trough on the door started rattling. The rats had somehow got into it and were gorging themselves audibly on the leftovers of my feast. They were fighting and shrieking, probably mad with hunger.

At first I thought of groping toward the door and beating them off, but I just couldn't make myself step to the floor. I silently scolded my feet, calling them cowards, and accusing them of deserting me. I'd remember this.

I started to fear that maybe I was going crazy; a sane human being doesn't argue with his own feet. "Take it easy," I said. "It's nothing, after all. Small gray animals, 'rats,' by name; I've killed a lot of such things back home in the pigsty."

But I felt the terror rising somewhere inside me, somewhere I couldn't reach. "You're acting as if they were lions," I said then, laughing. "Speaking of lions, this is surely nothing compared to what the martyrs had to face. They got shut up with lions if history tells us the truth. And you let yourself get scared by some tiny gray rodents! It's ridiculous, and you a latter-day descendant of an ancient warrior race."

Though I was very cold, my face and hands were sticky with sweat. I was a little frightened about that too.

But soon a feeling of easiness took hold in my stomach, and the corners of my mouth rose in the darkness. The feeling grew, and soon my stomach was hopping up and down with laughter. I wasn't afraid of the rats any more; I stuck a leg out in the air and asked with mocking courtesy, "Any little sweetie-pie out there who would like to swing a little on this?"

The distant clock struck twelve.

"The hour of the ghost," I thought, on the verge of bursting into laughter. I shook inside from laughter but secretly felt afraid to release it.

But soon I couldn't contain myself any longer. Eagerly and with a silent expectant grin, I put on my big shoes, hopped suddenly down on the floor, and stamped my feet wildly. As if I was observing it from a distance, I noticed a tingling in my scalp and heard my laugh.

The astonished rats scattered every which way. There were thuds when they hopped down from the tin trough and ducked into their holes. I could hear some screeching from the holes as they jostled each other to get in first, and then it was silent.

Groping for the bunk, I threw myself on it and nearly choked with laughter. The laughter had settled in my diaphragm; it was shaking fiercely and I tried to hold it still with my hands. Meanwhile, I went over the incident again and again, falling into new paroxysms of laughter each time.

I went on grinning and snorting for a long time, but finally I brushed the tears away from the corners of my eyes with my fingers. The rats, sitting expectantly in their holes, heard isolated explosions and bursts of laughter. At last it was quiet, and the pattering gray horrors regained supremacy in the cell.

They scuffled, fought, and screeched below where I was sitting with my legs updrawn. The laughter had left behind a strange emptiness inside me, which now began filling up with something new—terror for myself. "You can't stand this any longer," something inside me howled. "It'll split something in your brain, God help—"

I threw myself on the floor, ripping into some gravel-like piles with my hands. Gradually, one by one, my thoughts regained their old tracks and slid along on them. I grew calmer. "I'm still not crazy," I thought.

A rank smell flowed from a rathole just by my head. I surmised that the rats had been scratching together the piles of dirt I had just disturbed. "Since I understand that, I must be sane," I told myself in consolation.

And at last I felt the gentle strength of great resignation stream into my being. "Lie down and don't be afraid of anything," something called out from beyond incalculable expanses. "Someone has taken care of the matter. Be calm."

And just as the earth, the trees, and the skies were on my side when I was hunted through the forest, the darkness now began to bloom and give off a scent. From the little stone cell, I glided freely and securely wherever I wanted to in the universe.

I lay back down on the wooden bunk and soon fell asleep. I woke up once and felt a little weight on one leg. I kicked uninterestedly and heard the rat thud on the floor. At the door there was a continuous clattering noise in the tin trough. Then the blessed trance returned again.

I endured those four days in a curious state. On the second day, there must have been clearer weather outside; I saw the floor and the piles of gravel on it. I walled up the ratholes again with gravel and stones and listened in satisfaction for hours while the rats scratched themselves out to me again.

I was slightly proud of how I endured those days, and it struck me that one person was as good at enduring hells as another was at inventing them.

I sang all the songs I knew, and then I tried making up new ones. It was easy to slap a verse together, and I thought that maybe I had been born a poet. Happy and excited, I walked around the cell, reciting my poem aloud. It seemed to me more beautiful and more profound than any other I knew.

But when, white-skinned and red-eyed from the strong light, I was sent back to my old cell, I could scarcely control my great happiness. To sleep without the company of rats, close both eyes, and forget everything! True, I could still see rats even then, but I knew they were merely etched on my retina. Gray shadows sped rapidly across the floor, and on the second day I saw a rat sit blinking in the ray of light that on clear days between twelve and one fell diagonally through the bars, lighting up a spot on the cell floor.

The two-legged rat who was my work boss came in and hoped in his shrill voice that I would show them I wanted to be a good, dependable inmate now, one who brought honor to the prison. Otherwise, it was going to be worse, ten times worse. The rat was very close to the warden and would take care to report both good and bad news. He, the rat, had always been fair. No one could say otherwise.

Next came the chaplain. He touched upon my recent punishment in carefully chosen words. It was, after all, God who had sent it to soften a stone-hard heart. Pure love lay behind it. Number sixteen should remember that clearly. It was no pleasure for God to have to resort to such measures, either. By the way, had number sixteen read his colleague Vicar Salve's splendid little book? Indeed, but maybe with some prejudice. Otherwise, these matters are clarified there extraordinarily well.

And what about remorse? Did I understand that my prison term was a grace period to be deeply thankful for? God takes one aside for a while; He wants to talk individually to a man sitting in prison.

Since I was still thankful for my luck at being a prisoner again in a regular cell, I started to ponder what he said good-naturedly.

Did I regret what I had done? No, never as the chaplain meant; I regretted my actions as stupid only to the extent they had caused me suffering. And probably every criminal regretted what he had done in the same way. Besides, there weren't any criminals, just people with bad luck. No prisons would suggest that everyone who earned it both inside and outside the legal paragraphs should be locked up.

But the chaplain, who doubtless drew a fat salary, felt himself duty-bound to talk with a certain number of prisoners per day. "Pray," he said, staring at a huge, anatomically accurate drawing of a penis on the wall, "pray to the Holy Ghost for true repentance. Before that, number sixteen will not have peace in his soul and his life will be without worth."

After delivering that piece of advice, the chaplain looked at his watch and left, probably so I'd have a chance to put it into action immediately. But nothing came of it. I felt totally alien from heaven and its inhabitants, construed and exploited in a thousand cheap ways. No, I was young and my thoughts under normal conditions revolved around that part of earthly existence that would start the day the prison doors were opened.

Then they would see, damn it. I'd head for another country until the worst talk about me had stopped. At the same time, I would earn a lot of money abroad. It might, of course, take two or three years. Then one day, a well-dressed gentleman would step off the train at home by the summer-quiet station and take the inn-keeper's car home. I would buy the crofter's holding for my father, and people would have to notice that not all prodigal sons gulped down their father's fatted calves when they returned from a foreign land. . . .

The cell doors started slamming at the far end of the corridor. What was the matter? We had downed our mush, and it wasn't time for bed yet. Now came my door.

"Want any more mush?" the guard asked, sticking his head in.

"No," I answered in surprise. This was unfathomable! Never before had anyone been offered more food. In fact, I had often heard prisoners, like empty wolves, begging for more with pitiful voices, but all they ever got was gruff refusals.

The guard shut my door but hesitated outside it before moving on to my neighbor's. Then he opened it again, stuck in his head for the second time, and looked inquiringly at me. There must be something wrong with an inmate who didn't want more mush. He looked at me a while, his gaze hardening. "Don't try any funny stuff," he warned, shutting the door.

I was glad I had said "No," though my stomach expressed its displeasure by growling noisily. After a while, I heard the same noise again but then the mush procession passed by my door, number sixteen.

"What about this one, guard?" the prisoner carrying the surplus mush asked.

"The mush will be gone fast enough without our making a fuss over gentlemen," the guard answered disdainfully.

The head guard came in with the other guard and shut the door with an expression somewhere between contempt and formality. "Step over there and stand still," the head guard ordered, pointing toward the door.

Then they began a careful search of my cell. The leather and the bed clothes and the dark corners. They leafed through the Bible, the hymnbook, and colleague Salve's splendid little book, and finally searched my person.

"What are you looking for?" I dared ask without getting an answer.

Before they left the cell, the head guard asked with an angry glance over his shoulder, "You haven't found a knife and hid it, have you?"

"A knife? No."

"If we find you with it, you know what will happen to you."

"Yes."

Then I heard the procedure repeated in number seventeen. But how would an inmate get hold of a knife? Maybe a guard dropped one in the yards and someone snapped it up in an unwatched moment.

A yell suddenly forced its way out of the neighboring cell, and I heard a couple of muffled thuds against the wall. Then the yell of protest again and loud voices. The guards closed the door and conferred with each other as they walked silently past my door in the direction they had come.

Number seventeen walked in front of me every day when we returned from the walk in the yard. He was a small, bow-legged man with a large round head and eyebrows that had grown together. The day after the performance in his cell, he stopped for a moment in the door, turned toward me, and pointed to his face. Despite the distance, I could see that his lips were swollen and one eye blackened. Number seventeen rolled his healthy eye wildly and clenched his fist for a moment in front of him. That was supposed to mean, "They've given me this, all right, but damn it—"

The next day he was gone, and when he eventually came back again, his neck was skinny and white. He didn't turn around when, on his bowed legs, he searched through the corridor for his cell, and he entered it with submissiveness imprinted over his whole little frame.

He was probably the one who had the knife, or maybe he had made a wisecrack to the guards visiting him. The consequences could be the same in either case.

Monotonous message tapping in the prison language continued all through the nights. Over, under, and on both sides of my cell. Sometimes the challenging signal fought its way to me, but I never learned the language. The guard with the bushy moustache had said to me the second time he cut my hair, "All the better if you don't know it. Every week, several men get punished for that there tap, tap, tapping. But what was I going to say? Ah, yes, my boy's studies are going well. But you never know. . . . you see so much misery."

"What's he going to be?" I asked, although I had no interest in anyone but myself.

"We'll see. First he'll get his diploma. . . . then we'll see. . . . these are such strange times."

"Yes, but he'll probably become something in the world."

"You see so much misery," the guard repeated, blowing the hair out of the scissors.

Christmas Eve started well. The door was opened one extra time for you to snatch up a piece of white bread from the tin tray. Then came the usual ooze for dinner—a gray, well-thickened slop that, at best, might contain a chunk of potato or a couple grains of barley. But toward evening came the big surprise—the Christmas number of *The War Cry*[12] for each and every one.

"You get to read this evening," said a trustee walking past my door.

"But such a damn newspaper," a voice answered farther away.

Even so, it was a breath from a happier world outside, and I inhaled with pleasure the smell of fresh paper and printer's ink. And then there were pictures of women in it, far from enticing with their uniforms, kerchiefs, and guitars, but good enough to start fantasizing about. One was really healthy looking, with a face round as an apple. She had borne witness, too, in a precious letter:

The Lord commanded me to walk to a crofter's holding deep in the woods. A poor woman was ill out there. I forgot my umbrella. When I was half way there, it started to rain. I prayed in my heart to the Lord that He would stop the rain. Naturally, He could see I only had my thin black dress on. It stopped raining. The Lord heard his insignificant messenger. May He be praised. I met two men who swore at the dry spell that had kept it from raining. Then my heart rejoiced over the Lord's power, which He so gloriously reveals to his followers. Hallelujah. Hallelujah.

As the story continued, I learned that she reached the crofter's holding just in time to wrench the woman's soul from the claws of Satan, who had already arrived and was waiting, continually licking his chops. Hallelujah for that too.

I thought the clothes off the Salvation Army soldier and then she didn't look so bad. If I ever got my own room and one of them came along, then, damn it, I sure would. . . . They came around occasionally wanting to sell newspapers, and a friend told me once that one of them had spent the night with him because he bought the whole lot of newspapers from her. Thus should God be served with every part of your being.

12. *The War Cry* is the official Salvation Army newspaper.

It became clear to me now where my thoughts were all too eager to fly, and I thrust my foot in front of them. "Oh that's real nice," I said to them, "right on the night when Jesus was born." But my thoughts said they didn't give a damn about that. It probably didn't make any difference what you did in prison, and I shouldn't flatter myself by thinking I was the worst of all. I hadn't even drawn male and female bodily parts on the walls. They were already covered with drawings anyway; there wasn't room left for so much as a Vienna sausage more.

The mush was white that night or at least was meant to be. My clump came from the very bottom of the mush, where it had been burned solid. I didn't need a spoon since I could hold my Christmas porridge like a piece of bread in my hand. I ate while looking at *The War Cry*. There was a picture of a converted Negress from Natal who didn't look so bad. The missionary standing beside her looking so hypocritical had probably used her. And he was right to. There are a lot of good places in Africa, coffee bushes and banana thickets. Snakes and lions just made it more arousing.

The doors were opened a crack, a voice sang "Silent Night," and the organ played. That helped for a while, but when the bell rang for us to put our clothes out, my thoughts rushed back on their paths of passion.

After trying vainly to hug myself, I finally fell asleep. The Christmas night was cold and hard outside, but a helpful little dream transported me to the church back home on a summer morning. The sun was rising in the West under a ponderous blue cloud, casting a glaring light on the white church, the cross and the stones. The grass in the graveyard was a translucent green, and the sandy walkways were grown over again as if no one had been walking on them for a long time.

I was standing by the gate looking at the graveyard, not surprised that the sun rose in the West. But then I caught sight of a woman standing on a grave beside a meter-high cypress tree. The woman was simultaneously naked and wearing a green veil. But her eyes were the strangest of all. They were clear blue and didn't blink. When they met mine, I shuddered but couldn't tear loose my gaze.

Suddenly the woman crouched down and, without blinking or letting me go with her clear, hard eyes, began crawling toward me like a cat. She crawled between two rows of graves. With a violent shudder I broke loose and rushed toward her, my unbridled lust mixed with horror. When I was a few steps from her, she leaped up, stretched her arms toward heaven, and disappeared into the ground.

A tall plant with large soft leaves and two blue flowers now stood where she sank. I grabbed them—the cool leaves and the blue flowers—tore off my clothes, and crushed the plant to my naked body. All this was terrible and beautiful. The strange herb gave me the same sensual pleasure as the woman would have, and the two flowers stared intensely into my eyes. When I climaxed, they closed, and when I went limp, the large plant fell withered to the ground. The western sun moved behind the ponderous blue cloud, and a cold gust of wind blew by.

When I woke up, all was quiet and the prison was sleeping in the Christmas night. No tap, tap, tapping conversations were going on either. There was probably a half-moon out because the sky was shining such an ice-blue through the small window. Two little stars twinkled and my mind took off boldly toward them, but soon came rushing back filled with dread from the terrifying distance.

All gods had to be powerless there, I thought. Nothing but annihilation can exist in that freezing vacuum. Life on the surface of the earth was surely only a skin disease on the heavenly body, a fungus that would soon vanish. And what could I say about these creatures who busily jostle each other about for a few years, throw each other in prison for one murder, but reward each other for mass murder? Someone just says, "Think how nice things would be if these antisocial individuals didn't exist." The landlord's wife back home spoke German and wondered about anyone who could speak only one language. "Can you imagine anything worse than these half-cultured human beings?" She's dead now along with her culture and—oh, dogs are pissing on her grave, yes, dogs. . . .

There'd be stains on the sheet in the morning for sure, but I didn't give a damn about that. Those kinds of stains were probably on every prison sheet. What could they do about it? I was here already anyway.

The weather was mild on New Year's Day; the ground was bare and thawed by the wind. On the other side of the iron fence a little red nettle was shining, completely unharmed. I stuck my hand through and plucked it when the tower guard turned his back, and in my humble but vain way imagined that a higher power had allowed the nettle to grow in my yard as a special honor. I don't think that any of the other inmates got a flower on New Year's Day. I put the nettle in my water mug and kept it alive for many days.

And in half-hour doses I experienced the cold snowstorms in January, the water dropping from the roof in March, and the fragrance of the earth in April. The gentle showers of May sprinkled my close-cropped prisoner's head. Leafy plants smelling like hops shot up out of the earth inside the stone wall but bore no flowers among their masses of leaves. I saw the black cat again and tried to lure it over, but all it did was swish its tail indifferently again as it had done last autumn and walk on. Summer passed, and for the second time, I saw the plants freeze solid.

And one autumn morning the guard with the moustache came and said, "Get your things together and come with me."

My things were a comb, a mirror, and an almanac that I was allowed to buy with prisoners' aid, as they called it, during my first year.

"You're going to have a friend now," the guard said as we walked through the corridor. "You're going to be with a nice old man. Time'll go faster for you now too."

"Uh-huh."

"What was I going to say? Oh, yes, my boy is doing just fine. His teachers are real pleased with him."

"That's good."

"Yes. So here we are. You're sure to get along with the old man."

"Here he is," the guard said into the cell and closed the door.

I was standing in a little shoemaker's shop. A little old man was sitting behind a low bench looking through his glasses. He had a high but furrowed brow, a thick nose, and a full gray beard. It was the inmate who had limped in front of me through the yard many months before.

"Hello," I said.

"Yes, hello. You can sit down there right across from me. What's your name?"

"Lars Hård."

"And mine's Nordblom. You're going to learn how to repair shoes now."

The old man might not be so gloomy and pitiful as I had imagined when I first saw him. Once he got started, he kept talking.

"The days'll probably pass a little quicker for both of us now," he said. "You've probably pedaled the punching machine before, haven't you."

"Yes."

"Well, we can talk a little too. Tell me about yourself. Young people usually like chattering about themselves. But no lies. No need to lie."

I told my story as briefly as I could to my new cellmate.

"You see, you see, your life has started out well. These are mere episodes. A so-called criminal life sometimes can be better than an everyday, run-of-the-mill life. You don't realize such things before your life is drawing to a close. Once you've gone far enough along the road, you can look back and see why you had to go through so much misery."

Surely the old man can't be religious, I hoped silently. "And what about you, sir?" I asked.

"You don't have to call me 'sir.' No difference between us, even though some gray fluff is growing around my chin and yours is clean-shaven. Well, I'll tell you a little bit about me another time; but first I have to teach you to be a shoemaker."

"Is that what I'll be?"

"Yes, and don't be sorry about it. It's the most enjoyable work there is. All shoemakers become philosophers just as surely as tailors become busybodies and ladies' men. Comedians, too, even."

"So you're a philosopher?"

"Keep tacking down the sole I've got started here. Philosopher? Oh, yes, still one of the greatest. The proof is that I can tolerate life here in prison. But I bet you get claustrophobia."

"Yes."

"That's pretty stupid. You should have remembered that there's nothing to be scared of. You've already run into the worst thing that can happen."

"The worst—no, going crazy is probably the worst."

"You don't know that; you're not even half-crazy. The ones afraid of going crazy never do as a rule. They aren't talented enough for it."

"Ah."

"You think I'm always just flapping my jaws. Don't be surprised. I've sat here thinking through a whole bunch of things and haven't had anyone to share it with. I preached to a bluebottle fly for a month, but it died. I couldn't bring myself to talk to a fly's corpse."

The old man got up breathing heavily, reached into the window opening, and picked up a dry fly by the wings to show me.

"I had one too," I said.

"But naturally you didn't stoop to talk to it. There isn't any humility in the young; that comes later. The young just run around with their heads completely empty or completely full of animal drives. If that weren't true, you wouldn't be here, young man."

"What about you?"

"Me, yes. I see you—I'm here for something else. What was I thinking about? Oh, yes. How do you handle the girl problem here?"

"Girl problem?"

"I asked because I had a cellmate before for a little while. Religious, a little over twenty years old. He'd embezzled some money.

He was the kind who took care of himself, if you know what I mean, almost every night. It wasn't much fun to lie here listening to."

"Every night?"

"That's right. And as if that weren't bad enough, afterwards he would sniffle and ask God to forgive him for Jesus' sake. They must have a strange God. I don't know what was more sickening. The sin, if you want to call it that, or the prayer afterwards."

"I understand."

"Now I'm wondering if you're the same way."

"Me?" I answered with burning cheeks. "Go to hell! What about you, old as you are!"

"Ha, ha, ha, that was a long time ago. But what do you do? Do you dream?"

"Yes, I've done that."

"That's better," the old man said lightheartedly. "I used to do that too."

"And now?"

"Now I don't have those kinds of feelings anymore. They disappear, thank God, with the years," the old man said looking to the side. "Do you dream about the same woman?"

"Yes."

"What does she look like?"

"Clean, transparent veil, slender and with eyes like the devil himself. She crawls like a cat toward me even though she looks like a real lady."

"What do you know. I think a country boy like you should dream of some buxom girl in a hayloft. Well, does she slip away just a little too soon?"

"Yes, you know how it is. . . ."

"I'd sure like to have a dream like that," the old man said after a moment's silence. "But the woman should be small, not full-grown. And she should struggle. But why are you staring at my roll? You hungry?"

"Yes."

"You might just as well take half of it. You eat less at my age. I can't understand what good it does to give inmates a whole ration of bread in the mornings anyway. Most of them gulp it down right away and then don't have any for their food the rest of the day. But that's probably the idea."

"How long have you been in?" I asked the old man, chewing on his roll.

"Two years pretty soon."

"And how much left?"

"Four," the old man answered, laughing. "I'll be sitting here another four years, guarded from all the nastiness out in real life."

"Oh no! Six years! What did you do?"

"We'll talk about that another time," the old man answered evasively. "Knock a couple of heel pieces out of this bit here."

But I was curious about the shoemaker's six years. What could he have done?

"What did your old woman say?" I asked, though I saw he wanted to avoid the subject. "Or maybe you're not married."

"Oh, I'm married, if you want to call it that now. Yes, I'm married to a good-looking, fine girl."

"Girl—she must be an old lady."

"Thirty years younger than me. What did you just say?"

"God! Then . . . I mean . . . was she satisfied with only you?"

The old man screwed up his eyes and was silent a moment, but then he peered up strangely.

"I really should hit you in the mouth with the shoe tree here, but then I can lie to you as much as I want. The thing was that she didn't care either about me or about other men. She didn't need any."

"How the hell is that?"

"It's true. She wanted my hut and my garden; that's why she married me, an old, old man. I saw perfectly well she didn't like me, but I sacrificed my place so I could feel a woman's arms around my poor body. But I was tricked."

He looked up, knitting his white eyebrows. "Besides, what are you sitting there pumping me for? Staring at me like that? Watch what you're doing instead. Some shoemaker you'll make."

We weren't allowed to take our walks in the yard at the same time. When the old man had gone out for his half hour, I rummaged curiously through the cobbler's bench, and all the way back underneath I found a little piece of leather with writing on it. That woke horrible memories in me, and I dropped it like a hot potato. I glanced at the peephole in the door, but the wooden slat hung there mutely, and no one was staring in.

I hesitated a moment about whether I should pick up the piece of leather again and read it. Surely it could do no harm. What the hell harm could it do? The shoemaker wouldn't come back for a good while yet, and I could put the leather piece back.

But the writing was hard to decipher. The shoemaker might never have gone to school. I could make out a word here and there, but they were strange ones.

"What the hell is this?" I asked myself. "Why has the old man written it?"

The message made me somehow ashamed of myself, and I put the piece of leather back where I found it.

The old man came in, small and withered in his coarse prison clothes. He sat down by the shoe box and said, "The smell of spring's in the air today. Oh yes, you look at me, wondering what it matters to an old bastard like me. But I know sure enough where the real values lie. Most people stand in front of the store windows, staring with twinkling eyes at all the shit glittering inside, but how many do you think even see the trees, the skies, and the lakes? Well, the trees are good for making a fire, you can lie in the grass, and you can wash yourself with water."

The old man fumbled around in the shoe box and found a piece of tobacco, took a bite, and continued. "They let you buy plug tobacco here but no snuff or cigarettes. I used to use snuff; it clears your head better."

I sat looking out the window. Just then a white cloud burst in front of it, and behind its white edges I saw the eternal blue. "Look," I said, pointing.

"Just talk," the shoemaker answered with one eye on the window. "Before you came here you always had the blue heaven above you, but I really wonder how often you noticed it then. At most you said it was cloudy or clear. And it'll be the same way when you get out again. Man is more thankless than other animals, and if I were the earth, I'd move five hundred million miles closer to the sun and scorch the vermin off me."

"Five hundred? It's only ninety million miles to the sun."

"'Only,' you say. Are ninety million miles 'only' for you? But that's the way youth is: yeast, that's all. You ought to feel like a mosquito compared to that colossal distance."

The old man chewed with one eye on the window and said, "For a thinking man, the solitude here can be a blessing. I sit hidden away from everything, but infinite expanses open instead around me. A little isolation for everyone would save the human race, keep war and everything painful away. All misery comes from the fact that human beings don't stay long enough in one place for anything to ripen, turn clear, and sink to the bottom in them. They just rush here and there, tug a while on this, pull a while on that. Hand me the file."

The shoemaker thought a while, nodding approvingly at his words. "Yes, that's how it is. As soon as modern man senses serious thoughts coming on, he feels uncomfortable and looks for other empty heads to rub against. The resulting squeak is called a social life, conversation, and other things."

"Where have you read all those things?" I asked.

"Read—you think I can't think something out for myself? I've told you that it's the work here that turns you into either a philosopher or a fucking idiot."

"Or both," I suggested.

"Ha, ha, now you're getting it. But really, I think the smell of cobbler's wax has a favorable effect on the brain."

"Were you a shoemaker before you came here?"

"Yes, a parish shoemaker. How come?"

"Well, because the smell of cobbler's wax didn't keep you from ending up here, is what I mean."

"Just the opposite. It helped. When a man has thought about

something for a long time, he has to put it into action. In the beginning I let the wax odor affect only my feelings, but one day after my old woman had gone, my fate walked up to the hut. Everything worked out for the worst, and so here I am. And then? It's not so clear what I'm doing while I'm getting ready for my metamorphosis."

"You're probably just as afraid of dying as others are," I answered, looking at the shoemaker. He was completely yellow in the face and his beard was quivering. He couldn't have too much time left. Not that he was so very old, but that he had to have some kind of sickness consuming him. Only his eyes were sane and lucid.

"No, not completely, I don't think," he answered. "A rich playboy, for example, has a hell of a respect for death, but only because he's always pushing the thought of it aside. He never thinks about nature either. They go hand in hand, you see. The closer you get to the earth, the trees, and the skies, the gentler death seems. In the end only a quiet melancholy remains when you think about everything that'll be left when you're gone forever."

"You've sure got plenty of lubrication for your jaws. You should have been a minister or a preacher."

The old man glowered, took out the tack he was holding in his mouth, and answered, "Yes, I know I've missed my station in life. But what about you? Look where you've ended up."

"What about me?"

"Idiot!" the old man answered. "Take a look over here now and see how to wax a thread."

Outside, the heaven was a heart-gripping blue. The cell window was open a crack, and crisp drops splashed down from the melting snow on the prison roof. The factory sirens roared, and in the distance a mother was calling her child: "Rune, come back in; Papa's home!"

The smell of leather, the smell of cobbler's wax, a pillar of dust stretching from the window diagonally across the cell. Small, wizened, and untouched by heaven and the voice of women, the shoemaker squinted ironically at me, his tobacco forming two trickles from the corners of his mouth down into his beard.

Like the Creator of the universe, we rested on the seventh day from all our labors. Endless hours when the old man, the cell, and the cobbler's bench seemed impoverished and wearisome. In the morning, the worship service in the corridor when some inmates' voices in terrible hopelessness howled out, "A Mighty Fortress Is Our God," and a salaried voice talked about a coming life. He could keep it. I, Lars Hård, wanted to live now when the snow was melting and the women outside were wearing lighter clothes.

I heard voices through the window, and with great care and against regulations, I climbed up to look out. A goddamned inner wall stood there, blocking the whole view.

"Ha, ha, ha," the shoemaker laughed, "I knew about that."

"Why didn't you come out with it then? You usually sure aren't so scared of flapping your gums."

"Well-meaning, you know. After all, I can see how much you're suffering today, and so I thought a few minutes might just as well pass by while you were climbing up there. If you could just understand that the people talking out there think their hell is just as bad as ours. And if they don't have one, they go right out and hunt one up."

But the glands in my body were secreting unhappy fluids, and I loathed the old man's dry wisdom.

Outside the window the winter days passed by, each as much like the one before as hammer blows, filled with the smell of cobbler's wax, dreams of freedom, and shoemaker philosophy. I saw how little by little life was handing the shoemaker over to death; his yellow skin dried fast to his bones, and death's skull protruded more and more clearly. But he kept tacking, chewing tobacco, and sharing his wisdom with me. When phonograph music forced its way into our cell one day from a guard's quarters, he said, "Yes, if you could just understand that the people playing music out there really aren't very much happier than we are. Freedom seems like an extraordinary happiness from here, but when we have it again we won't notice it any more. We'll just glower and sneer and keep thinking we're having a rotten time of it."

"Not me."

"You too. If there were only two humans left on earth and they each had half of it, they would still fight until one of them was left lying there. Both would want the whole thing. But the one left living would still be unhappy with what he had."

"How come?"

"Because there wouldn't be anyone to be jealous about it."

The old man added a triumphant stitch to a shoe he was holding in his hand and started humming a song. It was "Blind Man Lindroth's Lament." [13]

Outside, the soft May rain was whispering down and the fragrance of tender grass rolled in little puffs through the window. I was alone; I had persuaded the old man to go to the prison doctor because of an old pain in his side.

"The examination didn't do any good," he said when he came back. "The doctor said it might be cancer, and then I knew I already had it. I'm not going to be operated on, but I can go to the hospital if I want. It can make you a little jittery, you know."

"You can still live for many years."

"I know. My mother had cancer, so I probably inherited it from her. Oh, yes, she went to the hospital, though she never really wanted to. She wanted to die at home in the old hut, and she should have been able to. Most old folks have a confounded respect for the hospital, but they die quicker there, mostly. Anyway, we drove her to the hospital. I was young, stupid, and callous, and Father was kind of worried, so we took her there.

"For a couple of months she had real bad pain, but then it let up. Then she sent for me. When I came in, I thought there just couldn't be any life in that thing lying there. It was a pile of bones covered with yellow skin, much worse than mine. She smelled like

13. A *rallarvisa*, a song sung by the men building the railroads in Sweden in the nineteenth century. There are two songs called "Blind Man Lindroth's Lament." In the first, Lindroth tells about becoming a beggar after losing his sight and one hand in a railroad accident; in the second, he remembers the pain of losing his first love.

82

a corpse; she had open sores. Wonder if I'm going to get the same thing?"

"No."

"The bag of bones opened its jaws and talked with my mother's voice. She said she was only going to live a week more at the most. And so she started giving me instructions about my old father and me.

"'It's probably best to sell the chickens,' I remember her saying. 'Pick up the chicken wire next autumn and roll it up. Put it in the attic so it doesn't stand around rusting.'

"'If you hire a housekeeper, be sure you find a decent person and not some good-for-nothing,' the old woman continued preaching at me. 'I should probably be here to have a look at her. A couple of men are easily taken in. Don't serve anything but coffee at the funeral. No one could expect a couple of men on their own to serve food. It'll be cheaper that way, too.' Yes, that was my mother, and now I have cancer too."

"You'll probably get better."

"You don't believe that. Obviously it's kind of depressing to die in prison. Especially when the sum of my life looks like this— small, ugly, one short leg, prison, cancer, and death. That'll be a nice little tidbit for the devil."

"Don't you believe in the devil?"

"I believe in everything. Well, well, so I have cancer. . . ."

At night after the bell had rung and all was quiet except for the monotonous wall telegraph, I lay awake looking at that bit of heaven visible through the window. It was a weak spring blue, and I knew from my almanac that there was a full moon.

It was on a night like this that the ground turned black in the hazel forest back home, a tepid gushing spring murmuring in the darkness. Around Easter time. Sometimes something could come like a breath of wild anemones, though there weren't any ready yet. Just a few white fluffy buds among the green and brown bunches of leaves under the hazel bushes.

"Are you awake?" the old man asked.

"Yes."

"I could tell by your breathing. When a man falls asleep, he breathes more evenly. Well, anyway, I'm just lying here getting used to having cancer."

"Don't think so much about it if it doesn't hurt."

"It doesn't hurt too bad right now. But next year around this time, I probably won't be alive. I'm not really afraid, but everything looks different now that I know for sure what the situation is."

"Doctors are wrong sometimes; it might be something else."

"Now that I have such a short time left, I'm starting to think about what things will be like afterwards. When I'm gone, it won't make a difference one way or the other that a lame shoemaker once lived, thought this and did that, but I still wonder if there isn't another place somewhere where other things matter more than they do here."

"Uh-huh."

"The way my life's been, it would be too damned awful to think that's all there is. Naturally, there might be incomprehensible things, some big translucent place where even I might mean something. A lofty, gentle being perhaps who counts invisible things in some unknown way. He doesn't know what punishment is, but he'll burn away the shoemaker, the prison, the cancer and everything, then talk with me so I know I've moved beyond all physical and disgusting things."

"Yes."

"Maybe you want to sleep. But someday you'll have to think about these things even though it seems to be a long way off now. It's unbelievable how short life is when you look back at it."

"Yes."

The moon had risen higher; a narrow strip of light fell on the cell door. It grew and finally the square pattern of crossed iron bars from the window sat clearly and coldly on the door. Then it moved to the left above the shoemaker's bed, and for a few minutes I could see his white beard, which occasionally moved. I wondered how long the beard would stay in the ground after the shoemaker was buried. The strip of light crept up the wall and gradually disappeared.

"The moon makes you think about graveyards and tombstones,"

the old man's voice intoned when it was dark again. "It's as if it shines brightest there."

"Yes."

"I'd thought about telling you why I'm doing my time here, of course, but it doesn't matter now. When cancer grabs hold of your body, it might be a good time to chatter less and think more. As I just now said, everything takes on a different light when you're standing in front of the last door."

"Yes."

"I'll try to shut up now. You're young and need to sleep. But I still wonder. . . ."

In June, the plants, heavy with leaves, shot up tall as a man from the warm earth near the stone wall, and their strong spicy fragrance hung like smoke above the prison days. A few bumblebees flew in from freedom and passed over the plants that hadn't bloomed, investigating them, then flew back over the wall with a disappointed hum. We trudged around the star, small, gray and insignificant, round and round in unfathomable meaninglessness, and above us vaulted the summer sky, eternally blue and boundless.

The shoemaker grew increasingly thin and yellow; he often sat bent over, moaning. But during those moments when he felt better, he talked as he had before, and his gaze was clear and fine.

"Now it's my turn," he said before he was taken to the hospital. "I can't get any help from the outside; I have to go into myself as deep as I can and see if I can find anything to hold on to. I have to tell you good-bye and wish you a little better than what I've had. If you're not afraid of ghosts, I'll come back and let you know what it's like on the other side. Ha, ha, ha."

I don't remember what I said in response; it was something empty and silly even though I would have given the shoemaker a couple years of my life, if that had been possible. When he was gone, I let the tears gush out of my eyes unchecked, and I took out the Bible to see what it said he could expect. Then I heard the wooden slate rattle, and saw an eye staring in at me.

What was he looking at? Did he think that now, once I was alone, I would start interpreting the Bible in a way that other Onan did? No, the Old Testament's heavy sexual atmosphere didn't interest me just now; I turned to the evangelists for something appropriate for a little lame shoemaker who had been doomed to death.

It was a day in June just after my herring and potatoes. My old friend felt the warmth of early summer and heard the lively hum of the insects for the last time. A warm gust of wind with the smell of cowslip in it might have blown past when he tottered across the prison yard. I opened the Bible, clasped my hands above it, and imagined that I had reached the God of the shoemaker, me and all wretches. I pointed out His absolute obligation to intervene in the shoemaker's case; I decided I didn't need to go into any detail.

At the end of July, we were both free. I had served my time and the shoemaker, against all the orders of the court, went off and died short of most of his.

I left the mush bowl untouched my last morning. I paced back and forth in my cell anxiously but failed to generate the overwhelming joy I was expecting. I was afraid of life outside the silent stone building.

At seven-thirty, the stately gray-bearded head guard came in and said, "So you're leaving today, are you Hård?"

"Yes, sir. Thank God."

"There are three other guys getting out today. If they suggest tagging along with you, don't let them. They're low life. Tell them to go to hell. I'm warning you for your own good."

"Okay . . . thank you."

"Come along with me now so you can get your clothes."

In the dressing room sat the three men the head guard had been talking about. I had let my hair grow out the last few months, but they apparently didn't care about such small matters. Their round skulls were clipped short.

I recognized one of them as the big white-haired man I had caught an occasional glimpse of and who I thought had thrown the leather bundle into my yard. His hair resembled pig bristles and grew over almost his whole head.

"I'm going out for a minute; don't get into any shit in here," the head guard said sharply and disappeared.

The inmate with the pig bristles glanced furtively at me. "How much dough've you gotten together?" he asked in a voice that was supposed to be friendly.

"Oh, sixty crowns or so."

"Damn good. Hey guys, first we're going to go get us a beer and when the restaurant opens, we'll get us a real drink and a bite to eat. Are you with us?" He turned toward me as he spoke.

"Okay," I answered hesitantly, thinking about the head guard's warning.

At the same moment, the head guard returned. He walked straight to the man with the pig bristles and gave him a shove that sent him flying into a corner. "You son-of-a-bitch! Did you really write your name and year on your cell wall?" he bellowed. "If I was doing my job, I'd give you a good beating before I let you out!"

He walked into a little room nearby and from there called, "Come in here one at a time; since you're all ready to go, you can have your money."

Pig Bristles glared at me through his slush-blue, fear-filled eyeballs. "That was a stupid thing to do," he said. "Now I'll have that old man on my heels like a nasty dog whenever I come back here."

I was amazed. Were there really people who took it for granted they would come back to prison?

I was the last of us four to get my belongings. The same nine öre and the jackknife with the broken blade. My handkerchief had been washed and ironed. All that was missing was two irreplaceable years.

Pig Bristles winked at me as the three of them walked out. The clock struck eight times.

It surprised me that there was no sign of the guard with the

87

moustache on my last morning in prison. But when the prison opened its jaws and spit me out, he was the first person I saw on the outside.

"I have my day off today," he said, "and I knew you were leaving so I came down. You're not much like the others who come here, so I thought I'd say good-bye."

"That was nice. . . ."

"And then I thought I'd make sure you didn't get mixed up with those chronic jailbirds who just left. They were thinking about just standing around here waiting for you, but I put a little life into them. Did you tell them you had money?"

"Yes."

"That was stupid. But we'll fool them, you'll see."

He followed me a while on a narrower road going up toward a hill and said, "Take this road here instead, and you'll get away from them. They're probably waiting someplace. If you run into them, who knows what you might be in for. What was I going to say—oh, yes, my boy, you know, finished school with the highest marks."

"That's really nice."

"Yes, but it's no use being too happy. You never know. Don't let me see you here again in any case," the guard said with a voice both sorrowful and rough. "Freeze and starve instead. If things get too hard, come and see me—not that I can do so much, but at least we can talk. Take this road here now and good-bye."

"I have so much to thank you for," I said.

"No need to. Just don't come back."

I stood watching him, wondering why he was sorrowful and gruff when things were going so well for his son. "You never know," he always said, not daring to believe in his son's future. But his gruff friendliness had done me endlessly more good than all the chaplain's sermons and visits put together.

In the crevices on the hill, little yellow hock weed was blooming, but everything was still too big and inaccessible for me. In two places the eternal granite raised its rugged head to the same height as the treetops' wealth of leaves.

Time seemed to have stood still while I was away; the late summer day was clear and full now, too. Small waves lapped the smooth foot of the hill down by the lake. By the road on a smooth, flat piece of rock, hundreds of people had carved their initials, and I thought about how much a person wants someone to talk about him after he has fallen silent—a child, a book, or two initials carved on a flat piece of rock.

Then suddenly a powerful feeling of homelessness came over me; I was reluctant to leave the surroundings of the prison. With shame and wonder, I felt drawn back to the huge stone buildings. They had been my home. I reminded myself how fortunate I was to be free, able to go wherever I wanted, but I couldn't muster any real enthusiasm.

The big city clamored in the distance, but I still didn't dare cast myself into it. I had my pocket mirror from the first year with me, and I saw my jaundiced prison skin in it. My eyes twitched anxiously and timidly, and everyone could surely tell where I had just come from. I couldn't bring myself to go home for years yet, if ever. In the country, people have good memories about cases like mine.

I turned around again to look at the huge stone building. It was sleeping with its long rows of black windows in the morning sun, and I heard the metal doors clanging as the star opened itself up for the first batch of prisoners to walk in. I still hadn't realized that I was free, that I could go wherever I wanted to. With a glance, I bid farewell to the prison, but I didn't curse it as I walked toward the hill.

I roamed around the area the whole day; I looked at my money several times and was glad to have it. It would surely last until I got a job on some foreign ship.

I had some coffee at a little cafe on a back street but couldn't tolerate it after two years' abstinence. The tables started waltzing around me, and I saw the waitress's sharp and disdainful eyes. "Are you drunk?" she asked. "Don't you dare throw up in here!"

I paid silently and staggered out. The girl came out the door after me and watched me go. She probably couldn't quite figure the drunk out.

I gradually found my way to the seaman's employment ex-change and stood hesitantly outside. Two men in tattered clothes stood with their backs toward the wall, warming themselves in the sunshine. Naturally I thought they were sailors. The tallest looked up a couple of times and met my gaze each time. "What are you staring at?" he finally burst out. "You lost something?"

"No—but I thought I'd ask—are you sailors?"

"Could be. What's it to you?"

"Yes, well, I thought about signing up, so I wanted to talk with someone who'd been out and knows what it's like."

The tall one observed me a moment in silence. "You going to buy us a beer?"

"No," I answered, thinking there was no hurry.

"Go to hell, then," the man barked, closing his eyes again. Maybe tomorrow things will go a little better, I thought, and walked on.

I walked around the whole night. Even though I had money, I couldn't get a room to rent. I sat in various parks and lay on a wooded hillside outside Stockholm for several hours. When I came back, the city was still sleeping; only the street cleaners were moving about. I tried to talk to a little man with a long broom, but he answered that I could go to hell and shouldn't try anything with a real native Stockholmer. He knew well enough what kind of fellow I was; he'd been around.

Although I had done my time, was now free and ought to be happy, I still walked around with a distinct feeling of uncertainty. I didn't dare ask anybody about anything, and so I roamed the streets. I barely had the courage to walk in and order a meal.

As a train clattered by, I came to a decision. I would go visit shoe-maker Nordblom's wife, Lena. He had suggested it himself before he was taken to the hospital. He carefully described how to get there—a hut to the left of the road, a big pear tree by one gable, a nice potato cellar across behind it. Flowers in the windows. She liked flowers, did Lena.

"It might as well be you as someone else," the shoemaker had said. "You can be sure to get some food and coffee; she's the kind that won't let a friend of mine go without offering him something even if she's mad at me. Besides the anger will go away once I'm dead. You can tell her that . . . that. . . . Oh, no use talking drivel. When it's over, it's over."

That's what the shoemaker had said. He was kind to me even though he would never see his hut or Lena again. He pretended not to be affected, but he grimaced worse than usual and made forced gestures. And a man's eyes run something awful when he gets so old. When he was young, he had better eyes than most.

I was the only one to get off at the little station. A sweaty station master in a linen coat cast an indifferent eye on me, and a couple of station workers uncoupled the last car on the train.

It was in the middle of haymaking, and haycarts and haycocks dotted the fields. The dust of the country road was full of straw that had fallen off the carts. One of the cart drivers waved his whip though he had never seen me before. It made me feel good, and I immediately looked on my future a little more optimistically.

I was supposed to take the side road. It was a country lane, rolling over some small hills. Gray stones, warmed by the sun, lay in the high, glimmering grass. Yellow bedstraw and wild strawberries next to an old gray fence. The intense smell of high summer, motionless in the sun. On the horizon, some midday clouds towering aloft, and one damned snarling airplane.

Off in the distance, I saw the hut with the pear tree by the gable. First the path followed a ditch, then wound dry and hot along the juniper slope.

There was no one in sight, and I thought there was no Lena at home. In that case, I might just as well lie down in the shade of the pear tree and wait a couple of hours. But then I saw some faint blue smoke coming out of the chimney. It was probably time for coffee in the country.

I stood behind some cherry bushes; I wasn't in any hurry. There was the cellar, a nice cellar just as the shoemaker had boasted.

Cheerful flies buzzed around me, settling occasionally on the cherry leaves. Their frail, aged wings glistened in the brilliant sunlight.

She'd have to welcome a greeting from her dead husband anyway, the woman inside. I couldn't imagine that she wouldn't. She had the little hut and garden all to herself now and all for nothing, just as she figured. She hadn't even paid for the place with the quick little transitory tickling feeling that the shoemaker had dreamed about for forty years. She should have. Surely she could have closed her eyes and pretended it was another man, if she found it distasteful. I would maintain that most authentic couples shut their eyes in the most intimate moments and pretend the partner is someone else. But no one wants to admit that.

That's what I thought behind the cherry trees. Suddenly I heard a door open, and I drew farther back behind the bushes. Through the foliage I saw a woman come out onto the steps. A large woman in a red-striped dress. She was no girl, no one could say that, but no old woman either. Her bottom swayed as she carried a pot toward the nice little cellar, but her legs were beautiful and her walk brisk. She wasn't bad looking, I can tell you that.

I thought about that long period of time without so much as the shadow of a woman, and I felt something moving inside me I had thought was dead. Who knew—maybe I could just stay here, heading for more peaceful days. I could marry the big, soft woman and hide in her arms from everything threatening and frightening out there among both people and laws. No one here had to know I had done time. With my talent, I might actually make good in a farm district like this one. Become the parish bigwig. The woman, who went back in with a full pot of cream, wasn't bad. "It might as well be you as someone else" were Nordblom's own words.

But it was high time for me to go in if I didn't want the shoemaker's Lena to drink her coffee all by herself. She could appreciate having a fairly good-looking man in the house.

I didn't see anyone through the window when I walked up and knocked on the door. The smell of coffee on the front porch made it feel like home.

"Come in," a woman's voice said, a little too hesitantly.

The kitchen was just about as I had imagined. A sofa, cobbler's bench, a ship's clock. The woman stood by the stove tending the coffee pot. The window was full of potted flowers, and the table was set with two coffee cups, a basket full of white slices of bread, some sugar, cream, and a half liter of schnapps. The afternoon sun washed over all of it and played in the crystalline schnapps. A man was sitting by the table. I looked at him and caught my breath. It was Pig Bristles from prison.

All of us stared—the woman and Pig Bristles at me and I at them. All that was audible in the beginning was the fire in the stove and the coffee pot rumbling, soon to boil.

"Hello," I finally said, but just then the ship's clock struck three clamorous beats. I couldn't hear if anyone responded to me. "I bring greetings from Nordblom," I said, trying to continue and turning toward the woman. She had a wart on her chin. I could see that Pig Bristles was starting to remember me, and his white-haired jaw drew into a gaping grin.

"But . . . but that's why *he's* here," the woman answered at a loss.

"That's right, I was working buddies with him for a while and did him a lot of favors," the white-haired man said.

"Me too . . . I mean, I was his friend," I responded but sensed that the white-haired man held the trump card.

Then it was quiet again for a while. The man furrowed his inch-high brow, looking angry. "What were you in for again?" he asked maliciously. "Didn't you kill a man, or almost anyway?"

"Christ in heaven!" screamed the woman by the stove.

"You don't have to be afraid while I'm around," the white-haired man said protectively.

There wasn't much for me there. I still didn't leave right away but looked around the kitchen instead. The sun was shining on the rag rugs, the flies were humming, and everything was snug and homey. There was an old portrait on the wall. "That's supposed to be Nordblom, I see," I said, pointing at the portrait and trying to start a conversation, but the woman looked at me in mute terror.

"Well, I'll be taking off again," I finally said, and no one raised any objections. The white-haired man only extended his grin over his broad face.

As I walked away from the hut, I felt two pairs of eyes riveted to my back, making me walk unsteadily; I took little wobbly steps as if I were drunk.

Instead of walking back to the station, I followed the road in the opposite direction. I kept swallowing as I walked but couldn't make the disappointment go down completely. It stuck like a lump in my throat. I had to pile contempt on her with a big shovel to force myself to go on.

"She had a wart on her chin," I said out loud. "And whiskers. Goddamned Pig Bristles can damn well have her. Nordblom was far too good for her, and so am I."

Then I ate wild strawberries in a rocky pasture and in every way felt more at ease than I did in town. At sunset, I sat on a warm hill but not so far from the shoemaker's hut that I couldn't see it. A dot of light glided to the cellar and back again, and I thought with some bitterness that now Pig Bristles was going to have his evening coffee and then . . . but naturally it wasn't all that certain he would stay with the woman. You always imagine more than you have to.

Besides, what did it really matter? The sun that had just set had witnessed millions of murders and all kinds of horrid things, but it rose and set anyway, bright and unaffected. I decided to be just like it from that moment on. I put a blue speedwell on my coat to remind me of my decision.

A narrow cove shooting into the landscape turned black after the sun had gone down. Some cows were walking by the shore, one with a bell on. Once the air had cooled down, you could hear every sound. I heard voices and rattling bottles from a farmyard as if it were right next to me. I sat on the hill's highest point, looking at the countryside round about me.

The wet-eyed melancholy of the summer night started rising from the meadows and fields after the sun had set. Like an invisible mist, it passed into my chest, mumbling about things that would never be mine but that might exist somewhere. As if the summer night didn't think I had suffered enough, it brought out a screeching accordion to accompany it; a boat glided out in the cove, and an old waltz, ennobled by the evening air and dripping red with heartache, ran across the meadows, sobbing, clambered up the hill, and threw itself on top of me.

I sat like a gray, trembling cornucopia of sensation on the hilltop, and I felt indescribable currents come up under me, pass through my body, and rise into the universe. The ordinary human part of me grew frightened, and after a battle with a set of religious and moral impulses, it started its mechanical countermovements to neutralize the current. When certain nerve bundles started radiating their tickling sensations, the pressure subsided a moment, but then built right up again. It excited particular nerve clusters to save its brain from those dangerous suggestions coming from unknown depths. It won, cast off generations of taboos, and said naked and laughingly, "Come on all you old spinsters of both sexes, souls dressed in coat tails, eunuchs with upraised index fingers, and take a look at one of you, yes, just one of you, who dares reveal his seamy side, sin openly on a hill after a thousand years of fundamental falseness. Do you know anything, by the way, about the shallow abyss called man? The eye of the ordinary fly has six thousand facets, and a cubic centimeter of sperm contains about a million possibilities for creating life. Dear Doctor, before you eat dinner, please write a certificate verifying, according to your opinion, the desirability of interring the person in question as being dangerous to society since he has shown superficial asocial tendencies. Your name here."

Afterward a dried-up, pitiable feeling of shame appeared, but I drove it off with a final, disdainful kick. Unlike most people, I wanted to look everything I did square in the eye. No apologies or deception in exchange.

Because of my countermove, the summer night lost most of its oppressive madness, and I was myself again. I got up and walked toward the woods I saw a little way in the distance. I saw blue-berries there, looking completely black in the night. I walked stooped over, eating them and snorting like a bear in the dust as I went. A broken basket lay abandoned in the twigs.

The time between midnight and sunrise was like a brass-colored curse with the mosquitoes' whistling hymn in the air and the cold dew in the grass. Now that I was free with no one hunting me, I couldn't latch onto that immense happiness that I knew existed somewhere beyond the great misery. An old, damned conformist voice inside me said I ought to go out in the world and find work, bend my back, pay taxes, and keep my mouth shut. Be one good, six-millionth part.[14] I could start with the Salvation Army's fire-wood yards and pea soup. I had been given a ticket to go there but had immediately thrown it away.

"Quack, quack, quack," said the ducks down in the reeds, and sometimes the bell tinkled when the cow turned its head. The cowherd had gone up among the trees to lie down; a motionless veil of mist now hung over the swampy shore.

A thought popped up, suggesting I should go down to the shoemaker's hut and try to hear what was happening in there, but I said an immediate and definite "No" to that. Then it suggested I might walk up to a farmyard and try to get something to eat, but I decided I would take the matter into my own hands when the time came. As far as I knew, there were still no laws against steal-ing blueberries. A serious gap in the legislation.

It grew lighter and lighter, and I knew the moment was ap-proaching when I would have to reach a decision. So I couldn't escape it, I sat with my back against a big rock in an enclosed pas-ture. Beside me was a dried cow patty and a rosehip bush with gray dewdrops clinging to the spider web. In the grass, a couple of ants that didn't make it home for the night crept slowly, rigid from the cold.

I understood now that the plans I had made for my future while I was in my cell were impossible. I would never come home as a gentleman from a foreign land and buy Father a cabin. Father, yes,

14. The population of Sweden was six million at the time the novel takes place.

and Mother—how come I thought so little about them? I quite simply hadn't dared to; the whole time they had sat as if frozen in my own Ice Age. I might consider going home. The hut was off by itself, and no one had to see me when I came.

My parents emerged more and more clearly from the murkiness of my memory; hints of them emerged from old hiding places. I saw my mother, who, like me, had so much difficulty in showing tenderness, but who always had an anxious look in her eyes when someone in the family was ill. Who scrimped, shared things equally with everyone, repaired things, cooked, and hunted bedbugs half the nights.

And Father, the cheerful, black-bearded man of Slavic race who was so gentle with the tiniest insect. Children and animals went to him completely of their own accord. Just then an image from my childhood popped up. We were tending the cows, Father and I, the estate's massive herd of cows.

Father lay on the hillside with the sheepdog beside him. I went up and plopped down in the clover that was in bloom and caught a bumblebee in my cap. It made two different sounds, but then managed to give me the slip. It flew away triumphantly, turned back, then flew back and forth again in front of my nose, humming defiantly. It did the same thing twice more before flying away once and for all.

Father lay in the grass, which was tall and shiny in the late summer. Bluebells and oxeye daisies were growing round about. Father almost never looked for shade; he would lie directly in the sun. I sat down quietly next to him and looked down at his big hand. There was a cricket sitting on it, and Father lay absolutely still so as not to scare it. The cricket fiddled on its thighs, turning its head as if it looked up into the friendly, black-bearded face.

"Yes, yes," Father said, "I hear you all right." And he laughed silently.

The cows grazed peacefully, the swallows caught flies just above the cows' backs, the sun scorched down, the grass and flowers were motionless. Afternoon. Far away a mower clattered along, and the dog whimpered in its sleep.

These and other images rose before me in the unfamiliar morning forest. A strong longing for home gripped me; I wanted to go home and tell Mother and Father that I had done this and that, but I had been made to pay for it, too. Not very often has anyone been made to pay for it as I had.

Surely I could stay with them until my horns grew out enough so I could butt heads with all the others over a piece of bread, a roof over my head, a bed, and perhaps a woman to go in it. All the terrible things that had happened to me would gradually fade, run like a black dog over the white snowfield of my memory only once in a while.

I stood up and guessed which way home was, said farewell to the shoemaker's hut and the possibilities inside, and set off on the road for home. Behind me the sun was rising, and it looked like a beautiful day.

Mercy

Introduction to Mercy

Since Rousseau, city and country have been uneasy bedfellows, the glitter and falseness of one often clashing violently with the simplicity and honesty of the other. That conflict plays a minor role in much of Jan Fridegård's work, but whenever city touches country, the latter is always much the worse for it. In *A Farm Boy's Road to Långholmen*, for example, the protagonist, lured to the city, ends up leading a criminal life and serving time in prison.[1] In *One Night in July*, the main character—a country boy—accidentally kills a strikebreaker from the city; and in *Sacrifice* (*Offer*, 1937), a *statare* girl comes to the city only to fall in love and die after an abortion. Light imagery attends the girl, and images of darkness surround her urban boyfriend. He is even called "Dark" ("Mörk").[2] As we follow Lars Hård through the streets of Stockholm in *Mercy* (*Barmhärtighet*, 1936), the final volume in the Lars Hård trilogy, we get a still more vivid sense of the big city's antagonism, and again that antagonism is life-threatening. Unlike some of his predecessors who wrote Stockholm novels—such as August Strindberg in his bitingly satirical *The Red Room* (*Röda rummet*, 1879) and Hjalmar Söderberg in *Martin Birck's Youth* (*Martin Bircks ungdom*, 1901)—Fridegård draws a uniformly damning portrait of the city. *Mercy* is thus a city novel most like in spirit to *King's Street* (*Kungsgatan*, 1935) by Fridegård's fellow *statare* nov-

1. Erik Gamby, *Jan Fridegård: Introduktion till ett författarskap* (Stockholm: Svenska bokförlaget, 1956), p. 27.
2. Erik Blomberg, "Stad och land i några nyare svenska romaner" in Blomberg, *Mosaik* (Stockholm: Tidens forlag, 1940), p. 169.

elist, Ivar Lo-Johansson.[3] Both authors roundly condemn Stockholm as a genuine source of evil, and Fridegård's book becomes perhaps the greatest Scandinavian "starvation" novel next to Knut Hamsun's *Hunger*.[4]

Stockholm turns into an endless, impersonal maze for Lars, who wanders from north to south, east to west, never finding a decent place to live, seldom finding a door open to him. After a short stay in a boarding house, Lars, one more item in society's refuse heap, is forced to inhabit a junkyard at the outskirts of town. Irony suffuses Lars's predicament because of the social aspirations that urge him back to the city in the first place. Unable to support himself at home, he becomes a peddler, hoping for financial and social success in Stockholm. But even that modest goal is met with disdain by the society he wishes to enter. He can earn no money and must turn to the state for help, only to find that without a permanent address he can have no financial aid. The city in *Mercy*, embracing as it does all of Lars's social experiences, including his imprisonment,[5] becomes the great symbol of his misery and frustration. It also becomes his crucible of suffering. His immersion in and ultimate rejection by Stockholm are vital components in his search for fulfillment. As Lars tries unsuccessfully to make his way from one milieu to another, he must face realities that can free him from the encumbrances of his own personality and the society that helped shape it.

The physical movement of Lars from city to country and back again is the visible and outward correlate of an inner journey, a journey Fridegård once again charts for us through patterns of imagery. In this final chapter of Lars's saga, nature, woman, and death are our major guides. If we look back at these themes in the first two novels, we will see a gradual leveling out, a gradual subordination of imagery to overall scheme. Initially in the trilogy,

3. English translations are available of *Martin Birck's Youth* and *The Red Room* but not of *King's Street*. For a discussion of the Lo-Johansson novel, see Alrik Gustafsson, *A History of Swedish Literature* (Minneapolis: University of Minnesota Press, 1961), pp. 517–18.

4. Gamby, *Jan Fridegård*, p. 78.

5. Långholmen is on the island of the same name north of Södermalm. See the map on p. 110.

Introduction to Mercy

some themes and images are so weighted that they call attention
to themselves. Learning is a good example. Lars tries to impress
everybody with the breadth and profundity of his knowledge in
I, Lars Hård. But his knowledge is sophomoric, tied to labels and
categories, not integrated into his being. Nature, too, rests very
much on the surface in the first novel. The descriptions are frequently maudlin, oversensitive reactions as Lars is characteris-
tically "startled" by the "silent, eternal, and rich" sunshine[6] or
moved nearly to tears by the thickets calling with "dark womb(s)
for some titillating sin" when infidelity hangs in "the fragrant
night air" (*ILH*, p. 34). In a flash of insight later, Lars himself remarks on his tendency to study his "own sensations respectfully
and marvelingly," counting them "singular and brilliant" (*ILH*,
p. 55). In *Jacob's Ladder,* he manages to integrate better both learning and his love for nature into his personality. If either one stands
out, it is nature, chiefly because of its absence.[7]

Nature in the last volume of the Lars Hård trilogy undergoes
yet another change, becoming at last merely part of the scenery, an
element in Lars's world assuming neither too little nor too much
importance. No description of nature is overblown; no reference
seems particularly exaggerated. Lars simply notices the wild chervils blooming outside his hut (p. 113), a wall of cloud mounting on
the horizon (p. 117), and the hawkweed and chamomiles flourish-
ing on the ditch banks and in the fields (p. 154). Nature is demar-
cated in *Mercy* neither by superficiality nor absence. It is merely
there, offering Lars the solace of its variety and beauty or seeming
indifferent to him.

The same phenomenon, the same resolution of tension between
Lars's view and the aesthetic function of the theme, occurs with
women, and the development of flower imagery throughout the
trilogy follows that resolution diagrammatically. Lars's callous,
manipulative treatment of women in *I, Lars Hård* provoked vio-

6. Jan Fridegård, *I, Lars Hård,* trans. Robert E. Bjork (Lincoln: University of
Nebraska Press, 1983), p. 20. Subsequent references to this novel appear in parentheses in the text as *ILH*.
7. See the introduction to *Jacob's Ladder.* Subsequent references to this novel
appear in parentheses in the text as *JL*.

lent outcries against the book; the flower imagery highlights his attitude. The first image dehumanizes both men and women: Lars likens the arms and legs of woman to the petals of a flower, and he implicitly compares the woman's lover, who will invade the petals, to a bee (*ILH*, p. 5). Even in his more metaphoric use of flowers, Lars forces the image so far from its referent that it turns grotesque and clinical: when he discovers he has taken a girl's virginity, he labels her vagina a "specimen" of "the red flower" and himself, the probing botanist (*ILH*, p. 15). The subtle poetry and playfulness of the carpe diem theme, from which the floral imagery ultimately derives, does not inform *I, Lars Hård*. Nor does it permeate *Jacob's Ladder*. But the imagery in the latter novel does not offend us as does that in the former. Lars dreams that a woman actually changes into a giant plant, which he then embraces. A curious image, in context it is nevertheless a natural identification of flower and woman.[8]

The convergence of flowers and women finally evokes the feelings and atmosphere appropriate to it in *Mercy*. Waiting quietly in the kitchen during his mother's illness, Lars and his girlfriend Eva sit down next to each other: "We didn't say much, but everything was different from in the forest—tremblingly ready and unavoidable. There was fire in her skin and in my hands. She sank backwards and opened up like the crown of a flower. Her face was more beautiful than I had ever seen it before; her eyes closed in fine lines, and her lips moved softly and only to answer mine" (p. 176). The image blends the idea of a flower with the ideal of romance and rises above the extreme precision of the image in *I, Lars Hård*, the one-to-one correlation between flower and woman, bee and man. The light touch that Fridegård employs here subordinates the image to the mood it is intended to create as the fragility, beauty, and delicacy of a flower are identified with the same qualities in Eva. This control represents something new for Lars, and his relationship to Eva is new, too. Her very name reflects that newness.[9] She is his Eve, symbolizing a new beginning, a new ac-

8. For an analysis of the dream, see my introduction to *Jacob's Ladder*.
9. Arne Häggqvist, "Fridegårds Lars Hård-stil," in Häggqvist, *Blandat sällskap* (Stockholm: Ars förlag, 1954), pp. 134–37, points out some of the allegorical ele-

ceptance of other human beings, of himself and his place in the
social order since she too comes from the *statare* class.[10]

Lars's physical descriptions of Eva coincide with the imagery he
applies to her. Instead of giving us an expression of pure lust, as he
does when he comments on one girl's "substantial accessories" in
I, Lars Hård (p. 29) or when he "thought the clothes off" a Salvation Army soldier in *Jacob's Ladder* (p. 70), the Lars in *Mercy* allows us to see and himself to feel the complexity of his attraction
to Eva. Watching her while they pick berries and fully appreciating
the suppleness of her body, Lars wishes he could have a woman
like her, "not just for the moment, but night and day, a woman
both intense and affectionate" (p. 160). Moving from the immaturity of his relationships in *I, Lars Hård*, an immaturity reflected
in the symbolic smallness of the blue-eyed girl he most admires,[11]
Lars reaches the mature Eva. She is an earth mother figure: strong,
unswayed by the opinion of her neighbors or even of her mother
about Lars, simultaneously sexual and nurturing. Such a balance
is absent in the first two books of the trilogy. Though we catch
Lars seeming to long for a woman like Eva in *Jacob's Ladder*, that
longing grows from social aspirations. He dreams of marrying
Lena, the shoemaker's wife, of hiding in the arms of the "big, soft
woman" and eventually becoming an influential member of the
community through her (*JL*, p. 92). Lars's ambition makes Lena
an impersonal object, a mere means to an end. In *Mercy*, Eva becomes an end in herself.

Nature and woman exert great influence over Lars and serve
clear and consistent thematic purposes in the trilogy, but they
have little of the overwhelming power of death, the reality that
Lars has the greatest difficulty bearing. He faces death three times
in the trilogy, once in each novel. In *I, Lars Hård* his confronta-
tion with it begins and ends with an 85-year-old man. He twice
discusses death with the old man, revealing a profound fear of it

---

ments of the trilogy, finally drawing a (not entirely convincing) comparison between Fridegård's methods and John Bunyan's.

10. Gamby, *Jan Fridegård*, p. 79.

11. Artur Lundkvist, "Jan Fridegård," in *Jan Fridegård*, ed. Artur Lundkvist and
Lars Forssell (Stockholm: Förlaget frilansen, 1949), p. 10.

both times (*ILH,* pp. 20–21, 39–41), a fear that prohibits him from feeling at ease either with himself or with nature. "The joy of the earth was intense," he tells us after the first discussion, but when he tries to force his way into that joy, "cowardly, sickly apprehensions cast their black shadows over everything" (*ILH,* p. 21). The juxtaposition of material here is telling: Fridegård wants us to see that death is inseparable from nature. Lars's fear of it, his inability to accept his own ultimate end, keeps him from having the equilibrium he constantly seeks. He seems to cling for a moment to a small part of that equilibrium the last time we meet death in *I, Lars Hård.* The old man's wife is dying, and Lars goes to comfort both of them (*ILH,* pp. 61–64). He still expresses fear of death, manifested in his frenetic actions after the woman dies, but he begins to see something besides his fear. He begins to perceive that peace, ineffable joy, is waiting on the other side of the boundary between life and death. In the old woman's inarticulate moan on her deathbed, Lars hears the music of the spheres. It is this perception that we see developed and amplified as we move through the trilogy.

The amplification does not happen immediately. Lars still expresses fear of death and eternity in *Jacob's Ladder* (pp. 16, 80), but the shoemaker's demise nudges him toward an acceptance of death as well as toward a more conventional religious experience and a more conventional desire for God than he has had before. After his friend dies, he searches the Bible "for something appropriate for a little lame shoemaker who had been doomed to death" (*JL,* p. 86). Not until *Mercy,* however, does Lars try to face death completely, this time as it takes away his own mother. The agony he endures as he watches her makes him realize that death poses no real threat to her (p. 175). It is inevitable, natural.[12] This realization also pushes Lars still further toward rounding out an eclectic kind of faith. He knows his mother is in good hands; he "had only to believe" (p. 175). The belief Lars expresses in *Mercy* is an ill-defined one, but it includes not only his faith in the mystical power

12. On Lars's relationship to death, see Sten Kindlundh, "Lars Hård, världen och evigheten," *Svensk litteraturtidskrift* 33, no. 4 (1970): 13–24.

of nature, which we first saw evidenced in *I, Lars Hård,* but also admixtures of folk tradition and orthodox religion. The owl, for instance, traditionally thought to be a harbinger of death, appears several times (pp. 12, 171, 174), sometimes to Lars's dismay, and Lars gives us two clear indications that he is more tolerant of traditional Christianity than he was in the past. He prays fervently by his mother's bed (p. 180), and he freely offers his hand to the minister who comes to comfort her, indicating that he no longer holds beliefs other than his own in total disdain. "You have Luke and John," he says, "I the spruce and the aspen. . . . Who knows whether or not we can light our paths with such different lanterns" (p. 167). Although Lars still condemns an orthodox religion based on the stern God of the Old Testament, he can at least incorporate some aspects of it into his personal belief.[13]

What Lars starts to reconcile unconsciously through a dream in *Jacob's Ladder* becomes more fully reconciled in his waking state in *Mercy.* His relationship to nature settles, becoming less self-conscious and urgent; his relationship to women also resolves itself. He no longer tries to exploit them, and he accepts—even wants—Eva for what she is. Most importantly, he at last starts developing a relatively coherent personal belief, one that can help him accept himself and overcome his fear of death. The adolescent struggles that engaged him in *I, Lars Hård,* the torment he experienced in prison in *Jacob's Ladder,* and the misery and suppression he endured in *Mercy* have been crucial in his quest for self-identity. Though Fridegård is too perceptive to imply that Lars has confronted his last demon, he does leave us with some hope. At the end of *Mercy,* Lars welcomes the new day promised by the warmth of yet another distant, unfamiliar sun.

13. For a slightly different interpretation of Lars's religious belief, see Peter Graves, *Jan Fridegård: Lars Hård,* Studies in Swedish Literature, no. 8 (Hull, 1977), pp. 5–9.

Mercy

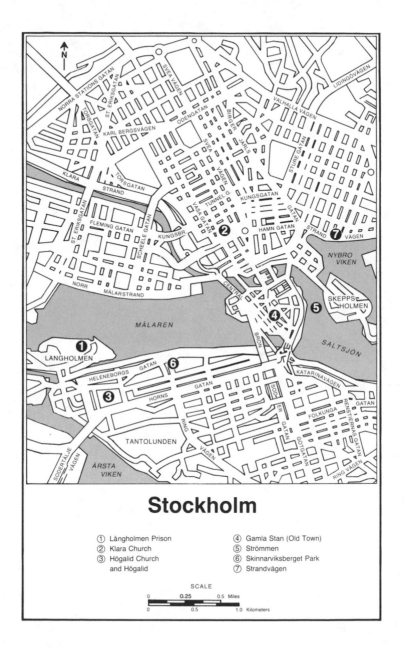

Stockholm

① Långholmen Prison
② Klara Church
③ Högalid Church
  and Högalid
④ Gamla Stan (Old Town)
⑤ Strömmen
⑥ Skinnarviksberget Park
⑦ Strandvägen

SCALE

0   0.25   0.5 Miles

0   0.5   1.0 Kilometers

On the third day after I, Lars Hård, was released from prison, I was almost home. I had slept in the woods for two nights. Although I had a little money left from what they had given me at Långholmen, I couldn't bring myself to ask for lodging anywhere. It was near the end of July; the days were a hot, sunny yellow, and in the afternoons thunder would rumble on the horizon.

My clothes were all wrinkled from sleeping outside, and I heard a couple of schoolchildren I ran into whisper "A tramp" to each other. It made me feel kind of bad. Although I had come from prison, I didn't want to be taken for a tramp. I pulled on my trouser legs to straighten them, moistened the stains in a spring, and brushed the dust off my shoes with a clump of moss before I walked up to the hut.

At the edge of the forest before I saw home, I heard Father out chopping wood. I recognized his way of letting the axe fall. I slowed down more and more, trying to swallow something that didn't want to go down. Father didn't look up, and I stood for a long time by the nettles a few steps in front of him. He talked to the logs now and then, scolding them if they slipped or were up to some other kind of mischief. I saw that a young maple tree by the log wall had grown a half meter and that Father had put a new handle on the axe.

He didn't recognize me right away; he looked up a moment, then split another chunk of wood before looking closer. The sun was on its way down and shone glaringly on my wrinkled clothes, it was almost evening and a swarm of large mosquitoes danced between Father and me. Sometimes the mosquitoes bounced up and down as if hanging from an invisible thread someone was pulling on from above.

In our family, we had never done more than shake hands, no matter how long we had been apart. We never wanted to show each other any tenderer feelings. I had thought a few things through ahead of time about this reunion, but all I could do was cough, swallow, and say, "Hello, Dad."

We took each other's hand; Father didn't look angry, but I saw he really didn't know how he should respond. It wasn't easy for him to know how a person in prison so long was put together, even if he was the father of the scum.

"How's Mama?" I asked, bending over to pet the cat rubbing up against my leg, completely oblivious to my having come from Långholmen.

"She's not what she used to be, but she's still around so far," Father answered. "Come on, we'll go in."

I didn't have a mother out of a novel who stretched her arms out toward me, fell to the floor, or screamed, "My son!" when I came in. She had aged more than Father, and I thought that some of the wrinkles in her face might well be attributed to me. She stood by the stove and looked a little surprised at the tall devil who came in after Father and stood silently by the door.

"Hello, Mama," the tall devil finally said. As I say, she didn't scream and she didn't put on any kind of act, but she said quickly and very intensely, "Lord, child, is it you?" and came up and took me by the arm. She stared up into my face, and I saw that her eyes were drab and clouded. Father looked at us, cleared his throat, and said that it was a damned shame when a person who had slaved away and done right all her life couldn't keep her eyesight till the end.

Neither asked me how prison had been; it was as if everyone was afraid of the very word. Mother made some coffee; Father and I sat at the table in our usual places. It got quiet and I fumbled anxiously in my pockets for something to show and boast about but found only my pocket knife with its broken blade. All I could do after two years' absence was hold it out and say, "Look, I still have this."

Father laughed a little the way he used to, took the knife, turned it in his hand, and said he'd be damned. Sure, he recognized it. Then things got quiet again, and I noticed that I emanated coldness from my hard face and the stigma of having been in prison. I probably would have stood up and gone my way, dangerous and disconsolate, if I hadn't seen a hint of tenderness light up Mother's half-blind eyes when I said something. And suddenly Father's tone became happy and friendly, and my throat constricted joyously with tears. I felt that I had avoided the greatest danger this time: going out into the world again with a petrified interior.

I walked out in the dusk with my heart full of gratitude. The woodshed stood out as before against the fading horizon in the West, and the wild chervils bloomed in dusky white clumps all around. The bats silently cut through the air again and again around the hut.

Yes, now I had to get a new grip on things. Believing in God on a still summer night was almost impossible, but once more I took the sky, earth, and trees as proof that if any of their power was in me it would now come to my rescue. Something would come of me because I had been struck flat to the ground time after time, flat as a fox skin on a board. I had a right to know the meaning of all this soon. How long would existence continue to hold its large fist clenched in front of my nose, I asked, but the night was murky, red, and silent. I was smaller than ever before.

I met some of my childhood friends during the next few days, and all of them were talkative and generous. They clasped my hand and said that once a person had paid for his crime, he was just as good as before, damn it. If anyone came up saying anything else about me, he would get a punch in the jaw from them.

I didn't dare go out in the district for a while. One day I saw two old women picking lingonberries hide themselves when I came wandering through the woods. What did the old hags think I'd do to them? Both had draped their shriveled-up bodies with rags, and that couldn't entice anyone, not even a prisoner from Långholmen. They took off anxiously on varicose-veined legs over the tufts of lingonberries, puffing through their wrinkled old snouts. The witches!

There wasn't any work now either. Father had asked at the estate one day, but the owner had said that he didn't want to have me among his decent workers. He took on a philosophical demeanor and said to Father that the bucket probably still had a bad taste in it. Hård's son should be glad he could stay on the property, he said. He could have been the kind who would forbid me to set foot on his land.

"Maybe you could be a traveling salesman," Mother suggested. "There are so many salesmen around here all the time." And she looked at me with concern in her drab eyes.

In my mind's eye I saw sewing machines, gramophones, and cream separators. No, that was too pedestrian; I needed a completely new and unknown product to offer to a surprised public.

The thought that I could be a traveling salesman cheered up all three of us. We looked in the newspaper and finally found a good advertisement. It was about tablets from Holland that were good for removing stains. They cost thirty crowns for a hundred boxes; if you sold them for a crown a box, you could earn a clear seventy crowns.

"I'll sell a hundred boxes in one day," I said, looking forward triumphantly to an incoming flood of crowns.

"Yes, if you take your bicycle," Mother said quite proudly by the stove. She was the one who had come up with the idea of my becoming a traveling salesman.

Father put up the seed money, I wrote to Holland, and in two weeks I had a carton of a hundred boxes. Every box contained three red and six white tablets as well as instructions written in bad Swedish. It was all mysterious and exciting.

The first day I destroyed my suit with the contents of one of the boxes, but the second day I set the other ninety-nine in the basket on the bicycle and set out on my way. Mother had put a loaf of bread, some pork, and a bottle of milk in a knapsack. My parents watched me happily and encouragingly through the window as I took the bicycle and pedaled off on the needle-covered forest path toward success.

I was careful not to stay in my home district. People there would either shut the door and close the shutter when they saw me coming or pity my continuing misery with veiled happiness in their voices and manner. Besides, I was ashamed of going around among people I knew, offering them those Dutch miracle tablets. I would rather have dug a ditch or chopped wood.

Out on the flatland the rye stood in shocks, and a mild hint of autumn hung over the yellowish-gray stubble fields. The larks took silently to flight by the edges of the ditches, and a frog lay crushed by a wagon wheel in the dust of the road.

I passed a *statare* tenement house, and two old women, each with a swill bucket in her fist, stopped their morning chatter to stare at me. They stared rigidly, tickled with excitement and forgetting to shut their black-toothed organs of speech. It was the first time the prisoner from Långholmen had shown himself. I didn't greet them but instead pedaled on, making the pills rattle in their boxes.

I rode a good bit into the neighboring district before I started thinking about selling anything. There were small enticing huts by the road, but I couldn't bring myself to stop and so pedaled furiously past. I tried to look like I was cycling for the fun of it and that any old thing could be in the boxes.

Finally, I slowed down and decided to try the next hut. I soon came to one, but there was a doghouse outside, and I thought with a kind of relief that maybe there was a vicious dog in it. I had my excuse for riding on.

I was several miles from home now and no one could know who I was. I managed to bring my bicycle to a halt, remove the carton, and go into a two-family hut. A younger and an older woman stared at me from the table in the first dwelling.

"Good afternoon," I said, my voice that of a timid idiot. "I—I was wondering if you could tell me how to get to Kulla?"[1]

Both women started talking and pointing. They walked out onto the steps with me, happy to have gotten off so easily, and the young one's supple arm directed me north. I thanked them and mounted my bicycle with an important air. At a bend in the road, I turned around and saw both women standing and watching me. They probably wondered why I had taken the carton with me inside if I wasn't some traveling salesman or peddler.

Something started gnawing inside me, but I defended myself by saying that it wasn't nice to fool poor people with worthless things. I could hardly use my suit after taking the spots out of it. Now I would intentionally avoid the small huts and sell the tablets to farmers and merchants. Priests too, in fact, who could afford to lose a crown. I would probably at least have time to sell enough so Father could have his working capital back again the first day.

Around midday I managed to get rid of one of the boxes, but the farmer woman grumbled and haggled down the price to seventy-five öre while pointing mistrustfully at the red and white tablets. It was the foreign name that had impressed her and made her open the drawer of her secretary desk to take out those seventy-five öre. I cycled on with some renewed hope.

Outside the next farmstead was another doghouse, and I didn't need any imaginary dog for that one. A big, gray wolf came toward me; it didn't bark but approached silently on its paws, sideways like a bluebottle fly, its fur standing up like a brush from neck to tail. The people on that farmstead could keep their stains as far as I was concerned.

Everywhere in the fields, men, girls, and children were working with forks and rakes. I envied them their clear-cut work; it was different from pedaling along the roads with phony foreign tablets in a box. This was no work for a young, strong, clever man. If I had anything at all in the box that could be of use or comfort to the poor, I probably wouldn't have pedaled past their huts. That's

---

1. Kulla is a small parish in Uppsala County north of Stockholm.

how I consoled myself, though there was a lot of hypocrisy mixed in with my little game.

I started to sense that the saleman's lot was harder than it looked, that it demanded something I lacked. I looked glum and withdrawn whenever I came into people's homes and couldn't talk about my wares. And my voice was, as I say, an idiot's, something right between half-thick despair and rough banter. The old women would look at me strangely and say, "No thanks, we don't want any."

Seen from home, the whole thing had seemed like a profitable and enjoyable ride. I would return in the evening, loaded down with one-crown pieces. But it was getting on toward noon, I was still pedaling past a bunch of farmsteads and huts, and the weight of three twenty-five öre pieces did not noticeably hinder my progress.

To regain my strength and courage, I sat down on a hill and opened the knapsack. Far in the distance I saw bundles of grain, evenly spaced, flying out of a binder that three horses were obediently struggling with. Then they stopped and the man took the horses away. He drove two and led one toward the farmstead and lunch. So it had to be twelve o'clock. A lunch bell rang from a farmstead I couldn't see beyond the hill.

It's no use denying that the ghost of misfortune stuck its tongue out at me on the summer horizon. Why wasn't I good enough to sell these boxes of tablets? Wasn't there anything in the world that I could do just as well as anyone else?

Maybe some people were just made to carry around the hedgehog of anxiety in their hearts. It tormented you and drove you here and there, from home to town to prison, from the soft arms of girls to praying to the empty universe on a gray rock in the night-silent forest after the girl had gone in and everyone was asleep.

It looked now like my afternoon business was going to run into a natural obstacle. Without my seeing it develop, a threatening blue wall of cloud was mounting on the horizon, occasionally rumbling protractedly. The sun was broiling hot, and wasps and bees whistled by like rifle bullets. A huge, shiny blue fly settled peacefully on an oxeye daisy beside me, which swayed a little under its weight.

In prison I had yearned passionately for the earth and flowers, but now when I sat among them they somehow shut me out. Of course, that was because the poor results of the morning had colored everything. If I had sold fifty boxes of the villainous tablets, everything would have made me much happier.

When the bell rang, generations of *statare* blood urged me to get up and start working again. The man with the horses came back, and from a distance, I saw him looking pensively toward the thundercloud, which had risen yet higher. There was a white bird silhouetted against it, and I guessed there was a lake between the cloud and me. It might not move across the lake.

I came into a hot fir forest that had no huts in it and that would never come to an end. The birds had fallen silent and an aspen tree by an abandoned clearing stood motionless, looking as if it were listening for something with every leaf. A mountain currant bush glowed on top of a pile of bricks that had once been the stove of a hut.

I got into a couple of huts when I came to the end of the forest, but no one wanted my tablets now in the blue-black atmosphere. In one hut an old woman sat with a hymnbook opened in front of her and, with a face rigid with old-time pious respect for the thunder god, watched the cloud that was getting closer and closer. I was right up next to the table and could see a hymn beginning, "On Sinai stood the Lord our God. . . ."[2]

The thunder rumbled again and the leaded window panes rattled. The Dutch tablets didn't fit in there and I walked toward the door. The old woman looked rigidly after me, moving her lips.

In the next hut, fear of the thunder made the people eager to talk. A young stableboy in blue work clothes pointed at the tablets and said they looked pretty funny. But he didn't have a suit; otherwise he sure as hell would have bought a box. He walked around

2. A hymn written by F. M. Franzén in 1812. In the first verse, a stern God stands on Sinai in the midst of fire, smoke, and thunder, admonishing sinners.

in blue work clothes on Sundays and weekdays and was none the worse for it. He looked around and said he didn't give a damn what people thought.

"Don't swear when the thunder is carrying on like that," said a middle-aged woman by the stove.

After the people in the hut had kindly advised me to find another stock-in-trade, I rode off. By then the thundercloud had moved in front of the sun and a cold wind preceded it with the message. The grass lay down before it like a shiny carpet. I had the wind at my back, and the rubber tires sang from the speed.

Suddenly the thunder roared right over my head. The clap sprang to the side and stopped farther away with a questioning metallic peal. Then a whispering and murmuring started up behind me, and big drops started falling on the dust in the road. I thought about going up to a hut a little way from the road to seek shelter. But a white face in the window stopped me.

I imagined myself from the thundercloud's vantage point, wondering what I would look like from there. Like a little, floundering spider on the gray threads of the country roads? The cloud probably considered me scarcely worth hurling a bolt of lightning at.

The rain increased and I had to head for cover. I found a reddish-gray barn and took shelter under the gable. Flashes of lightning cut constantly through the darkness, and there was a crashing and scraping over my head. At first I was afraid a lightning bolt would strike the barn and get to me, but the tenet from peasant philosophy that you couldn't escape your fate made me stay. If God wanted to burn up one of his wandering and tormented insects with a lightning bolt, He was welcome to. The lightning bolt and the insect belonged to him throughout eternity, amen. He could have the Dutch tablets into the bargain.

The harsh rain whipped the ground at an angle; the thunder rumbled and was answered dully by a new cloud hovering on the horizon. I stood by the barn for an hour; then the sun came out and the road began to steam. A rivulet had dug down into the pebbles and was still rippling among them.

Still hoping to salvage the day, I took off with the courage of despair for the farmsteads. But now the people were haughty and rebuffed me. The storm had passed and they were still alive. You didn't think they were afraid, did you? This weather was nothing. No, you should have been here in ninety-three during the summer. . . .

The district was sunny but cool from the rain. I rode past a little farmstead that the lightning had struck and set on fire. A burned cow raised its huge stomach among black logs; the smell was rank. Some men stood around the church firepump talking about the storm as it drew away.

Anxiety stuck like a big block of wood in my being, and I didn't dare enter any hut. I stood outside instead, witnessing the struggle between the traveling salesman and Lars Hård and the salesman's surrender. I pedaled mile after mile, occasionally resting on a hillside. There was a pathetic hole where the box of tablets I had sold used to be. Ninety-eight red and blue boxes rattled scornfully whenever the bicycle hit a bump or a pothole.

I decided to stay away until Father and Mother had gone to sleep. In the morning I would explain to them that the countryside wasn't the right place for my business talents. I would cycle to town and sell all the boxes in no time. People in town have more need for a product that removes stains.

Although deep inside I knew I was wandering a hopeless road, I felt somewhat relieved. I had at least avoided disappointing the old people the first day. I agonized over the thought of Mother looking out on the pine-needle path, blinking her dull eyes, and Father reading the newspaper, yawning, glancing furtively out the window, and saying with feigned indifference that business must be going well if I was taking so long.

Oh Jesus, it's so hard to be a human being.

When it got dark, I turned the handlebars south, homeward. It was still several miles away, and my parents wouldn't sit up and wait. I had the night to come up with a plan.

It was pretty dark when I rode along the path to the hut, and the unsold boxes scolded me again when the bicycle bounced over the tree roots. The hut was asleep—Mother had drawn her red-striped curtains over the windows. An owl on the roof of the woodshed was outlined against the night sky. When I approached, it flung itself into the air and flew silently into the forest.

I sneaked into the kitchen. Mother had left the evening meal on the table. There was a pan with fried potatoes and pork in it on the stove, still warm. The cat lay on the bed linen on the sofa, and when I started to eat, it woke up, peered at me, then jumped up on the table, enticed by the smell of pork.

Instead of lighting the lamp, I opened the curtains. The night's gray light fell in on the table. The trees outside were motionless; a hedgehog waddled across the yard, a moth struck against the window like the hand of a ghost. The cat sat beside me, its cold, expressionless eyes seeming to look out over the ages and guard the silence itself outside the window. Inside the bedroom the clock whined and struck eleven. Then a thought flew, hard as a stone, against my head and I put the knife and fork down. "You eat so matter-of-factly, you devil," the thought said.

And then I realized that I always came home and sat down at the table after my misfortunes—matter-of-factly, as the thought said. I always came home tall and empty-handed, and I always looked toward the table once I got inside the door. I jumped up in a rage and went out.

Deep in my being, I heard mumbling about something that I finally ought to do—that I should have done a long time ago. Hesitantly and tentatively, something said that it would probably be best to make an end of it—yes, I knew myself how things were. I walked quickly, suppressing the voice as long as I could; I didn't dare let it be heard. But it was alive in my depths and held the door open for me, a black, cursed door perhaps, but one that might lead to something for someone like me.

I walked trembling from my own excitement; I was both performer and spectator. The owl had returned, and like a moment before, it flung itself out into the air and flapped into the darkness.

"You're pretty stupid if you're afraid of me, you damned owl," my lips said while my thoughts clambered around wretchedly in the brushy neighboring area. Everything I had been through and thought had been settled came creeping and hopping after me on my crooked life's path; it would all catch up to me soon and crush me with its combined weight. The recent years in prison came rolling along like a black-red mist, and out of it all the other disgusting things stuck up their snouts.

I almost ran through the miles-deep brush forest and saw in an endless distance a desolate moon, red as fire, going down, the treetops lacerating its underside. Hell with it.

I stopped on a steep hill by the cove. The hill had ledges like sofas, and I had played there hundreds of times as a child. I sat down on a ledge, and for no reason at all, the memory of an old man hovered before me. An old man who sat resting on a rock in the woods on his way to death in the poorhouse. I walked past as he plucked at the rock with his arteriosclerotic hand, saying it was on that very rock that he and his old woman had decided to get married fifty-three years ago. Now the woman was dead, as I knew. She was at rest.

The grass was growing tall and shiny around the rock as it does in the late summer; a mild breeze came, the old man's voice quivered in the clear, eternal air, and I wanted to howl with compassion for everything.

But I was the one whose life was at stake now. I tried to sidestep the issue yet again; I wouldn't let myself come to grips with it. Below the steep hill the waves came wandering black and smooth, and every second or third one let itself splash timidly against the hill.

Then something said in small black letters that there, under the smooth surface of the water, lay escape for Lars Hård, who was good for nothing. I had known from way back that the water was deep.

A mosquito bit me on the hand, and as soon as I started scratching myself, I thought, "What are you scratching for? The itching will stop forever soon. Rotting skin doesn't itch."

Then the tears welled up in my throat, and out of an immense

distance I heard something like a flute playing, delicate and sorrowful. By the reeds near the shore left of the hill, something was
splashing vigorously, and I could hear a strange sound like a dull
moan. The night grew more intense around me, and the far shore
stepped forward in a clear, black garment. My head reeled, and I
saw a naked man come out of a spruce alcove and then go back
again. Then the darkness swarmed around me, raining down in
black flakes. Somewhere the flute was stifled.

I hadn't thought about getting up yet, but I did get up and said
the old nagging prayer I used to pray—"If You exist, then You
have to understand all this." The coward in me quivered and still
hoped that somehow someone would interfere. Then came a still-
ness and once more I heard the delicate splashing of the waves. It
seemed to have grown lighter, but that couldn't be.

My practical side, which was almost always quiet, came clambering forward, wanting to assert itself before it was too late. It
took on a steady demeanor and said that I could leave my clothes
on the rock. We were the same size, Father and I, and he might
have use for a suit. I slowly took off my coat and trousers while a
cool night breeze tickled the hairs on my legs.

I was expecting that something unique would present itself,
some completely new and weighty kind of solemnity before the
end. Something terrifying but magnificent. But my other side slid
away from my thought—I could follow myself only until my
struggling stopped and the last bubbles rose to the surface of the
water, but then a mist concealed the rest.

I didn't yet dare walk out to the precipice; black water had always scared me quite a bit. I sat beside my clothes and a skinny
little thought poked up in my head, asking timidly if this was
really necessary, if there wasn't some other way. But that didn't
help; my fatigue and the disgust I felt for myself were just too
great to allow me to go home to my parents and boast about tomorrow with the hedgehog in my chest. Say that things had gone
a little poorly today, but tomorrow, by God. . . .

As I sat there, the mist lifted from the landscape that I sensed
lay on the other side of life. Although I couldn't make out any
details, I felt warmth and friendliness rising above it. But my deci-

sion to go there just like that suffered a painful and disturbing blow. The skinny thought grew fatter and fatter and said more and more forcefully that the only way I would mature and build myself a footbridge to the peaceful land was through misery. If I took a footbridge now, right into uncertainty, no one knew where I might end up.

"You're probably just a coward," said Lars Hård the failed salesman. "You don't have the guts, you son of a bitch."

But the new voice answered meekly that it was probably more cowardly to shorten the path than to follow it all the way to the end.

I had heard that before, I thought to myself. You rationalize whatever you do.

The idea that you ought to endure everything deeply pleased me. It wasn't just my cowardice in the face of death that made me think about whether I could tolerate as much as anyone else—if not more. Standing on my head in the lake down here probably wouldn't make my parents any happier, even if I gave them no happiness alive. Or would they brighten up when someone came to tell them that I was lying here among the reeds, rocking with the waves?

Then the moment of dark repose before the turning point. For the second or third time in my life came that weak harmony or light, I don't know which. It sung, lit up, and spread itself over a meadow or a plain in my being, and suddenly I had the strength to heave the whole burden away from me. An immense consolation burst out like a gigantic flower in the night air; I stood up sobbing and pulled on my trousers.

"That's over," I thought.

And I felt a huge hand above my head; it could strike me or shelter me, I didn't care. I also felt a large eye blinking warmly and observing the insect Lars Hård that it might put to some use.

But the road was still long and hard. The thought of meeting my parents' disappointed eyes almost nauseated me, and again I started looking for a way out. Well, whatever kept me from fleeing across to the black uncertainty could just as well get me out of this, too.

Now that it had grown a bit lighter, coots started chattering in the reeds. A night mist hung brooding over a little inlet. The underside of two banks of clouds, miles long, was turning slightly red in the East. The insect on the rock hunched under the millennia, which like the shadow of a brontosaur, flew before the sun when it came.

Things soon went back to normal around me again, and my thoughts danced in the usual ring. The surface of the water shone hard and tin-gray in the morning light. The spruce trees rose in countless clumps on the other side of the cove, one like the shadow of another, as rigid and unified as German soldiers. Two cows were standing on a sandy point of land. The mist, dissipating, glided like a wisp of smoke across the surface of the water.

The fact that I'd been off playacting for a few hours hadn't changed anything back home. Night had returned to the sofa, and the grease had solidified in the pan, but that would have happened even if I'd been floating under the water's surface as the first rays of the sun were groping out.

Though I hated the city and expected no good from it, I knew I had to go back again. I didn't ask why; I carefully put a little pork and bread in a paper sack and stuck it in my pocket. Then I wrote a letter and laid it on the table. I wrote that I was riding to town to sell the rest of the pills. People had more use for such things in town. I was leaving early and didn't want to wake them. Good-bye for now. I'll soon be back or will write and send back the money Father had shelled out.

The sun was level with the treetops and shone on the woodshed, the nettles, and the wild chervils. A ray of light fell in through the window and shone on the district newspaper, on the knothole in the table, and on Father's glasses. I tore myself violently out of the protecting calm of the shabby room and walked out with the box under my arm. After I had ridden a while, I saw the cove glimmering among the trees; I saw my night rock bathed in pale morning sunlight, and I pedaled on, asking out into the air, "What are You going to have me do now? Can't I get out of this soon?"

It was afternoon when I approached the city. I had seen thousands of people during the trip, busy with harvesting work or their hands full in some other way. Why did mine always have to dangle empty and clumsy? Most of the people I met had a confident expression on their faces: "I do what strikes my fancy, and so I can tell anyone to go to hell." As usual, I stood outside every group, not fitting in anywhere.

On the outskirts of town I ate the last of my pork and threw the rind in the ditch. I clenched my teeth and set off into the resounding hell. I walked the bicycle, thinking it was too late in the day to start any business. But in the morning the real day would begin.

After thinking a while, I walked to the pawnbroker and got fifteen crowns for Father's bicycle. I saw him tie a number tag on it and wheel it into the storeroom. It followed along like an old cow next to him, submissive with bent horns. But I wouldn't abandon it; I would redeem it as sure as. . . . Well, I didn't know anything that was too sure anymore.

With the box in my fist, I walked out to rent a room. I got one from an old lady who rented out by the week. There were already two men in the room and I would pay eight crowns a week. There were three beds and three washstands, and each washstand had a chamber pot and a wash basin; there was a chest of drawers, and we each got one drawer. On the wall was an oil print representing St. Genevieve [3] with a hind in her arms.

The old woman showed me the room and hoped in a piercing

3. Eighth-century Duchess of Brabant, who was falsely accused of adultery and condemned with her newborn son to death. They fled and lived on roots and deer's milk in the wilderness. One of the most famous pictures of the saint and the hind is an etching by Ludwig Richter (1848).

voice that I was a proper sort. She only rented to proper people. She was actually of "better" background but had lost her money and had to support herself. But she had always led a proper life.

I properly laid a ten-crown note in the "better" old lady's hand and received two crowns in change. A roof overhead for a week ahead of time wasn't so bad a future prospect for Lars Hård.

It was hard to sleep in the room; both the other men emitted every possible sound with an accompanying change in the room's atmosphere. I lay thinking about whether I had seriously thought of drowning myself the night before or if I was only trying to fool myself. Make myself important in the only way left. Now that I was in the middle of the scramble for food again, the solitary rock and the still surface of the water seemed distant images from another life.

When cars turned corners, light came into the room, lighting up St. Genevieve's gentle face and the hind's nose. One of the men lifted his head, listened, and started masturbating. Then he lay there, sighing, and lit a cigarette, which glowed bright and dim, bright and dim.

The next morning I could see that both my roommates were peddlers. One, the oldest, sold condoms, books, and French picture cards to the sailors on the boats; the younger one sold shoelaces. They talked business and looked a little disdainfully at the farm boy and his antistain tablets.

After whispering to each other a while, they started talking menacingly, trying to scare me into paying for their morning beer. I didn't say a word, just rolled up my shirt-sleeves to wash, and they soon fell silent. They were puny little men and together probably weighed about as much as I did by myself.

I should have had a little satchel to carry my wares in, and I stood for a while by a display window looking longingly at one but didn't buy it. Something told me to be frugal with the money I had left. I wandered about for a while until I found a street that looked nice and quiet. I wanted most to go where workers were living in small apartments.

You couldn't be too pushy and ring at people's doors too early if you wanted to sell anything. I waited inside a cafe for an hour and then started with the first house at the end of the block so I could take them all in turn. System is a prerequisite for success.

Not many doors were opened at my hesitant ringing, and those that did open shut again before I had a chance to say a word about my tablets. But in one place a younger woman stepped to the side so I could come in. I walked bewilderedly into the hall.

"I have a completely new Dutch product here for removing stains," I began and clawed inside the box. The woman looked at me in surprise.

"Aren't you from the gas company?" she said. "No, no, I don't want anything!"

And she pulled the door open indignantly for me to go.

A gray-haired lady with a pointed bonnet and a pointed nose bought a box from me with disinterested friendliness. I could see she wanted to buy herself a ticket to heaven by doing good deeds. By limping along in the Master's footsteps on that last stretch of road. A big German shepherd stood behind her, snarling threateningly and spoiling the image of the thousand-year kingdom he would otherwise have created with his lavender-scented mistress.

I held out courageously for several hours and sold another couple of boxes, though at a reduced price. I walked up endless steps; endless peevish "Noes" and slammed doors rang in my ears toward evening. But the following day I would go to Södermalm[4] and try there. I had a feeling that the people there would be a little easier to talk to.

In the evening I went back to my room and put the box on my bed. My roommates weren't in, but a half-empty liter bottle stood between their beds. I went out again and spent a couple of hours in a park and at a cafe. I walked about with a country boy's confidence inside that something unusual would happen to me here in the city, something beautifully climactic. The sun would rise over my inner landscape.

I thought I heard my roommates talking when I walked into the

4. Södermalm is the large, now very fashionable, mainland area south of central Stockholm. At this time, it was an industrial area filled with slums.

hall, but it became immediately quiet. Both lay curled up in their beds sleeping when I came into the room. I looked into my box and saw that a lot of pillboxes had disappeared. When I emptied them onto the bed and counted them, I found twenty missing. I looked mistrustfully at the men, thinking that they were snoring too well to really be sleeping.

While I took off my clothes, I wondered what I should do. The anger rose thick in my throat when I heard the phony breathing of the two little men. I couldn't wake them and accuse them of having stolen from me, but in the morning I would sure give it to them.

Eventually I lay down but shot back up again. I had put my feet down into something cold and clammy, and when I turned on the light again, I saw that both of my sheets were soaked through down at the feet. With silent rage I walked across the floor toward the closest snorer, and I saw the skin tighten over his cheekbones when he heard me coming.

"Don't lie there faking," I said in a voice hoarse with anger. "Get up and I'll show you!"

But he didn't move and I couldn't hit a man who was lying down. He was puny besides. I stood there, looking down on him while I wondered why there should be so much damned wickedness in that little conglomeration of skin, bone, and stubble. The object breathing heavily down there between the dirty sheets might walk around in a stoop with his shoelaces for a few years more, drinking up his profit, but then he would vanish like me and everyone else, be totally gone. Couldn't he just as well be nice while waiting for his end? But he was probably the same as I was: he confused himself with the earth's axis in significance.

I lay down again, drew my legs up, and gradually fell asleep. In the morning I was awakened by the peddlers' loud talking about their exploits and business. Their talk was directed and forced, probably to keep me from starting trouble about the previous night's events. I wanted most to keep quiet now too because of the oppressive atmosphere of the city morning, because of a new disconsolate day ahead, but then the peddlers might think I was afraid of them. I'd probably lose the other boxes, too.

"Which one of you swiped those tablets out of my box here yesterday?" I asked threateningly. The men started swearing. Was I accusing them of stealing? Was I calling them thieves? Prove it, you bastard!

"Well, who else has been here besides you two?" I asked more feebly.

That didn't concern them. But if I wanted, they would get a cop right away so I could repeat my accusation in his presence. Well, speak up! If the farm boy didn't know any manners, they would arrange for him to learn some.

Police, I thought, and saw in my heart a severe commissioner who would move his corpulent index finger along the columns in a big book. "Lars Hård . . . oh, yes . . . here, released from Långholmen in July . . . well, well, my boy, let's see."

And they might lock me up again for something I could have done without knowing it. The law books are like Satan's spider web and can ensnare anyone they want to. Maybe it was forbidden to remove the stains from society. My two roommates had things a little better; the one held on to Mother Sweden with shoelaces and the other with condoms, all of the finest quality, according to them.

"Just say the word if you want a cop in here," shouted one of the little men, grabbing hold of the door handle.

Then I said that maybe the old lady had come in and taken a couple of boxes. The day before yesterday I had a pile this high here in the box.

Well, then I certainly shouldn't be attacking them. They would fix it so I'd get mugged in a dark corner some night. Did I think they were born yesterday?

I took my diminished wares under my arm and left. I walked on a street that was long and morning-empty; the sun hung in the east entrance, sweeping along the stones in a cool pale red. There were silent, distinguished homes here, and bourgeois piano sounds floated from the windows of a couple of them.

But it was Södermalm I would take the stains out of today. I would walk off to the silent hovels on the hills. I longed for the rugged granite and the clumps of grass clinging here and there.

I had a strange feeling when I saw the masses of leaves on Långholmen[5] again. I was drawn to the place; I sensed the bittersweet smell of hops wafting over the wall from the plants inside growing tall as a man. If I listened carefully, I could hear the trudging on the walkways inside. Let me see, yes, the second batch was out now.

I felt a peculiar, suckling longing for the shelter of the prison yard and took off in terror toward the hills. The guard on the wall stopped and watched me. But he had never seen me in anything but prison dress and couldn't recognize me.

It didn't go much better in Södermalm than in the northern part of town; people were pretty much the same. Around lunchtime, the salesman's energy was almost totally gone, and he started offering the boxes at half price. That moved things along a little better, but the dinner at some joint took the whole day's income.

Deep down, I could see I wasn't going to surprise the world as a businessman either. That meant finding something else. Maybe I should visit the employment agency. I'd heard it was no use, but maybe I might have some luck. I had no background except the regiment and Långholmen, but they both served important functions in society. Can you think of a state without regiments and prisons?

I went there the next day. I had to force my legs forward when I saw the groups of workers outside. Pride made me go to the business department; I thought I could count and write pretty well.

After a couple of hours waiting, it was my turn. There was a line, and every time a bell rang a man got to go in. I lied about my place of residence the last few years; I said I'd been working in the country. I couldn't just stand there and tell them I'd been in Långholmen. The man filling in the form for me said I should request a reference from where I had been.

I got a card anyway, a red, folded card that I had to show four

5. The island of Långholmen is adjacent to Södermalm, so Lars passes by it.

times a week to get stamped. I asked if there was any hope of getting a position, but instead of answering, the man pushed a button that made the bell ring again.

I either had to find myself a phony reference and risk a new guest appearance on the green island or tell the agency I had done time there. I couldn't do either and knew I was having my card stamped in vain. But an older man in the waiting room brightened up the morning a little for me.

"You ought to go to the unemployment office and ask for relief," he said. "It's not much to live on, but take it anyway, damn it."

He told me what I should do and say. They would try to scare me away in all kinds of ways, but I shouldn't give in. The bold would get some help; the timid got to starve in whatever way they pleased.

So said the older man, writing down the address to the office responsible for my parish. I walked over the same day and found a long line. It cast skittish and unwilling eyes on every newcomer. The men looked as if they were thinking, "Here comes another bastard to fight over the crumbs with."

Most of them were badly dressed and smelled of rags. I stepped in line and perhaps smelled like old rags too. Still, I was the best dressed of the ones I saw.

It went slowly. Everyone, it seemed, had to confirm his life story for the girl at the counter window. How would it turn out for me when I had to lie about the past two years?

A fairly well-dressed stout man came in and walked up to the empty counter window with no clerk. "Hello!" he called in an importunate voice, and a woman walked up to him.

"I need help," the man said in the same hard tone. "I have an old lady and three kids at home but nothing to stuff into them."

"But you've moved," said the woman, thumbing through some papers. "Yes, you've moved to another place."

"So what? I'm still listed here, and here I'll get some help. And by the way, let me talk to a man," he finished disdainfully.

The woman turned red in the face and fetched someone who was probably the office manager. The man repeated his request.

"But you've moved," the manager said.

"I didn't come here to talk shit, I came here to get help," the man broke in. "My old lady and kids are at home starving, and I know where I'm going if you don't do anything about it."

"Come into the office, and we'll see what we can do," the manager said.

In a little while the man came out. When he walked past us in line, he triumphantly waved a bundle of ten-crown notes. "That's how you handle those bastards," he said, and the woman in the counter window cast an angry glance after him.

But we stood there silent, clumsy, smelling of rags, and Swedish in every way. It was finally my turn.

"Name," asked the girl.

"Lars Johan Hård."

"Address?"

"I've had temporary accommodations," I answered. "But now I have to move since I can't pay the rent any more."

"You have to give us an address where we can visit you and check over all your data," the girl said impatiently. Behind me the line was murmuring in dissatisfaction over the delay.

"But when I don't know where I'm going—"

"Next!" the girl called.

"But I have to have relief," I said, trying to be as self-assured as the other man had just been. "I don't have anything to live on."

"You have to give an address then."

Disconsolate, I gave the address of the hyena of a landlady I had boarded with a week.

"You'll get an answer in about three weeks," the girl said. "Next!"

I sold the boxes I had left to a paint dealer for ten öre a box and lived on that for a few days. I had started spending the nights in a junked car. I had seen that a few slats were missing from the fence around the junkyard at the edge of town, and I crawled in there every night after it had grown quiet and empty. I slept in an old Chevrolet, which in turn was resting after many years of creaking.

The nights were still pretty light, and there was a cover in the car that I pulled over me. I took off my coat and pants when I slept so they wouldn't get too wrinkled. I dreaded the day when I'd start looking like a bum.

I was never discovered or driven off; the only thing that happened was that I found a skinny girl lurking around my flat one night when I came home.

"Want a little company?" she asked when I stopped.

"No, thanks," I answered. "Why do you want anything to do with me anyway? Be on your way and mind your own business."

She swore and walked leisurely away. The lantern shone on her skinny legs in their light stockings.

What would I do with her, I thought, watching her disappear behind a tin shed. Who knows what the old whore might have. Life's bad enough anyway.

It would take some time to tell you about the long September nights in the junked car—how countless times I pulled on the cover to get it to reach in every direction, how my long legs got doubled-up and numb, how I walked round and round the car slapping my arms in those gray chilly mornings. But, anyway, I got to go wherever I wanted when the daylight came, and that was worth a lot compared to what I had before.

I went and got my card stamped every day and overcame my great disgust for the dark area filled with hardened, derisive men.

I often sat in a graveyard on clear afternoons. Peace had come to a halt above the old slabs in the grass, and Klara Church's[6] huge steeple bathed in the quiet white sky or eternal blue.

Even out there, among the stones of the sleeping people, walked a half-withered female body trying to hire itself out to those sitting on the benches. She sat beside me and tried to catch my eye, but I looked away, whistling indifferently. Then she walked over and sat down by an older man in work clothes on another bench. After talking a while, they got up and left. Two little old ladies, who looked like pug-dogs, watched them go with wrinkled repulsion.

An old gentleman with a white moustache put flowers on a hundred-year-old grave. He took his hat off and bowed to the

6. Klara Church in Norrmalm, built in the sixteenth century.

tombstone. A scornful laugh flew down from a workshop window, where you could catch glimpses of a few blackened faces. The color rose somewhat in the old man's face, but he didn't move and didn't look at the window.

Right in front of me was a poet's grave from the eighteenth century. The Swedish Academy boasted in gilded words that they had raised the memorial.

So it goes, I thought; the poet starved and died in poverty, hated and persecuted for the sake of his genius. When he's dead and can't decline the honor, they plant the sign of their impotent Academy pride right above him.

There may have been genius in that association at one time, I thought further. But now it's a club of old upper-class geezers from the most diverse spheres who admit their brothers and friends. May the Devil join them! I, Lars Hård, saw farther than most people, and no one had better try messing with me.

Klara Church thrust powerfully up into the blue, and in the ground at its feet lay three poets, a royal mistress, some ministers, and a mass of common people with children jumping and shouting on their graves.

After three weeks of life surrounded by barbed wire, I went to the old woman I had boarded with and had given the address for. She chastised me first for my effrontery in giving out her address and then tossed a gray letter at me.

The letter announced in a bold print that I should present myself at a certain unemployment office a few days later and bring along proof of age and the employment agency card, stamped four times per week.

That night it started raining. The tin roof didn't reach out far enough, so the drops drummed monotonously on the car's hood. A tree stood behind the fence and occasionally shook in the cold, sending huge drops splashing down. A streak of light fell diagonally from the lantern, and I saw some large, prematurely yellowed leaves flutter down and settle in the rain-wet mud in the streak of light. I shook with cold the whole night and saw before me the kitchen back home. A fire was glowing from the stove vent, and the red-striped curtains, warm and peaceful, were drawn down.

I walked a few turns around the Salvation Army's pea-soup line one day but didn't have the courage to join it. The looks from the line flew at me like rocks, driving me off into the side streets. The smell of soup followed me alluringly for a few steps, but I went on. Outside town, I ate my daily portion of bread accompanied by the smell of cooking from the houses.

Then the day came when Mother Society took her lopsided son on her knee, not to scold him this time, but to feed him. I arrived where I was to receive my unemployment benefits in plenty of time, but there was already a line. The place had unpainted wooden stairs and iron railings to keep the creatures to be fed from going wrong. Behind the counter windows you could catch glimpses of white hands belonging to some kind of lucky demigods who handed out money and blue coupons for rough, work-hardened hands to clumsily grab hold of.

Some distance in front of me in line, I saw a man who was half a head taller than the rest. The point of his moustache stuck out when he turned his head, and there was something familiar about him. Suddenly he turned half around, and I recognized him, although I couldn't believe my eyes. I gave a start, and my heart began beating harder: it was the prison guard who had been so nice to me.

He hunched up his large frame as well as he could, hoping like me that no one would recognize him. I wondered if he had seen me coming and remembered who I was. How could he have ended up here on the dole after such long service to the state? Probably, against regulations, he had let his friendliness toward prisoners go too far. How could he, with his big, gentle heart, have let himself become a prison guard anyway when the world is so full of contradictions?

I saw him walk across the floor toward the steps, and while he walked he took out his wallet and stuffed in the dirty ten-crown note he had just been given. He didn't look up, but I recognized him. Just to be safe, I held my hand up in front of my face in case he should look my way. Not for my sake but for his. But maybe we would run into each other even so; after all, we both did come from the same parish with the big two-steepled church on the hill.[7]

By now the prison guard's son, full of hope, had probably finished his studies, I thought, as his father's back sank down and disappeared on the stairs. No, now was not a time for compassionate people, I knew that well enough. It was a time for square jaws and hard elbows. The prison guard was still holding himself up straight, but he would be pressed down more and more by having to sign in at the unemployment office; by assistants who dug in his private life with hard, dutiful fingers; by oppressive traipsings from one source of help to another, all with the same counter windows and the same answer inside the windows.

And in the shadow of all this, countless children grow up, a stamped generation: "Papa's down at the unemployment office, Daddy has gone to sign in."

"Next!"

I was next, and when I had confirmed that I was Lars Hård, I got approximately four crowns, I don't remember how many öre, and six blue coupons, good for some grub at Norma's.[8]

"What do you say we hit some beer joints together," said a voice beside me. A man my age and tolerably dressed kept step with me, looking at me expectantly.

"But I only got four crowns for the whole week."

"Who the hell do you think got more? But almost all of us on the dole buy a drink and a little grub on the welfare money. When the unemployment office makes its payments, it's as crowded in the beer joints as when the Baptists have a convention. What the hell! It's sure better to feel like a human being one day and have a still shittier time of it afterwards than to walk around half-starving the whole week. Besides, you have the coupons."

It felt nice to have a human being beside me who talked directly to me and who didn't sit behind a counter window. But he was

7. Högalid Church in Södermalm (built between 1917 and 1923) is renowned for its twin steeples. Its parish includes parts of Södermalm and Långholmen.
8. One of a chain of restaurants.

going to the restaurant and if I wanted to feel the radiance of a friend for a while, I had to go with him. He said something about schnapps, but I felt my mouth watering for a beefsteak with a lot of potatoes.

The restaurant was on a hill, and the autumn's intensely colored flowers burned in boxes and flower beds. Fat women with swaying behinds served us, and my new friend's eyes lit up at the two drinks in frosty glasses. I fingered my money uneasily and didn't have any real joy from the feast. What if the money didn't hold out?

We laid bare our lives for each other and probably lied a good deal. The two schnapps enveloped the nastiness nearby in a soothing fog, and we moved to the future beyond it. He was expecting an inheritance from an aunt, and when he got it he would start a freight business. I would be his manager, I could bet the devil on that. His old aunt was pretty tough, but he hoped the cancer would get the best of her.

My future wasn't as concrete as his there at the restaurant table, but I looked out in the universe, saying with innuendo that soon, damn it. . . .

"We can go to my place and clink a couple more beers together," my friend and future employer said. "But you have to leave before my girl comes home. She's the one who pays for the room, see—she works."

On the way there, my friend kept laying out his life. Yes, he lived with his girl, but she was kind of nasty, and that's what he had to put up with if he didn't want to ship out. She was the one who paid the rent and bought the grub.

"You have to leave when I give the word," he said anxiously as he unlocked the single room on Rat Alley.

"I don't give a damn if I go in at all if that's how it is," I said, foggy and pigheaded.

A steep, dark, stone stairway continued upward, and a cat with evil eyes sat hunched on one of the steps. A hundred-year-old, inveterate smell of poor man's food hung oppressively over everything, and old ladies, dressed like those back home in the poor house, peeked out a little bit everywhere, furrows of mistrust carved permanently into their snouts. Moonshine, yelling, a feeling of belligerence.

"We're not drunk, so it's all right," my friend said. "The thing is, last week when I got my welfare money, we had some moonshine, two other guys and me, and we got drunk and puked all over the rug. So you can imagine what it looked like when she came home—puke and ashes everywhere."

"No wonder she was mad."

"That didn't bother me. But she slugged me one right in the jaw, and that's going a little too far. A girl!"

"She did?"

"I was pretty damned mad and tried to hit the table, but I was so drunk I hit the flowerpot instead. It busted and I cut my hand. Look!"

He held up a huge fist with a couple of nearly healed scratches on it.

Shortly after we sat down, bragging back and forth to each other, a key was put in the lock. My friend quickly put the beer bottles behind his chair and wiped the table off with his hand. I looked tensely toward the door, expecting a tigress on two legs or some other nightmare creature. So I stared without saying hello when a little lily-white being came in and closed the door behind her. She had big blue eyes, and they swept through the room, searching down into every nook.

"Hello, Marta," my friend said, a little forced. "I brought a buddy home, a damn good guy. We're stone sober."

"Yes, of course, that's just fine," the flower answered, stretching out her child's hand. "As long as you behave yourselves, I won't keep you from bringing a friend home."

I was mostly quiet after she got there, and it looked as if she might like that. My friend bragged on, glad that it all had worked out without an explosion. I had some coffee and it got pretty late before I left.

"Where do you live?" my friend asked, and I came up with a street name at random.

"That's a hell of a long way, and it's raining besides. Marta, could you make up a bed on the floor for Hård here?" my friend asked benevolently.

There was some hesitation in the girl's blue eyes, and that was enough for me. I got up and said I wouldn't hear of such a thing. I liked walking and roaming about at night, especially when it was raining.

"You're a funny devil. Do what you want then," my friend said.

The lily had a gentle expression on her face when she reached out her hand and said I was welcome back.

On the first day I couldn't bring myself to use the food coupons, but I gave one to a guy asking for handouts. That was when I was hovering around outside the food joint. Later I saw him through the window eating the coupon food and reading *Politiken*.[9]

He looked content and I thought that he and I were different breeds. They'd find my skeleton in the wrecked car before I'd go begging for my food. But that guy there was the kind who would make it. He'd get a job soon, ride on a firm's bicycle, protrude his clumsy lips and whistle "Kalle Scheven's Waltz"[10] or whatever the latest hit tune was.

I, Lars Hård, learned in the city that the boundary between the solitary human being and humanity coincides with the latest hit tune or craze. A terrible symbol of emptiness following along with us through the ages. Ninety-eight percent of the people hum or whistle the tune while their eyes gape, round and empty, at their surroundings, asking, "Can't you hear we're keeping up with the times, we're delighted to be part of the herd?"

Through the joint window I saw a man and a woman dressed in mourning clothes. They ate and drank with idiotic expressions on their faces that asked whether everyone saw that an old lady in

9. *Politiken* is the chief newspaper for the Swedish Communist party. Its full title is *Folkets Dagblad Politiken* ("The People's Political Daily").

10. Popular song by the still-popular Evert Taube (1890–1976), one of Sweden's greatest song writers.

their family had died, and so they were a little bit better than others. "We're grieving, damn it, look at our mourning band!"

I also saw how people with new shoes kicked up their toes as they walked and how new capes and coats seemed to stop by themselves in front of the reflecting windows. I saw that all the better because I glared at my own reflected image when I caught a glimpse of it.

I returned occasionally to my new friends, and the girl became more and more tender toward me. Soon I couldn't even look up without meeting her gentle blue eyes. But the man grew correspondingly morose even though he never found me showing off for the little woman. When he was drunk, he came out with angry, indecent words.

I stayed away for a few days, and when I came back, she was alone, just like in a story. She said with disgust that the man was probably at a beer hall. I thought about leaving again, but she laughed and said that I was as stupid as I was tall. If I thought I was too good to stay and drink coffee with her, well. . . . And she looked at me with a twinkle in her eye.

It's clear that the girl and the coffee made me feel good, but I still wasn't comfortable. She started talking about her man, and her voice got harder. He had no character and she couldn't stand the kind who couldn't say no when they had to. He frequently came home drunk, and she was totally fed up.

"If only he were like you," she said, playing with my fingers. "You're never drunk and I think you value things."

"I'm no better than he is," I answered. "Maybe worse. If you only knew what kind of devil I am."

The girl took my other hand and played with that instead. Then she said that she could see in my face I had a strong character. I looked so determined.

You poor mite, I thought. Långholmen has drawn my face taut and you think it's proof of character.

But her words did me some good, and I glanced over at the mirror for reinforcement, but it wasn't where I could see myself in it.

I probably wouldn't have cared so much about a little girl's affection before, but now it penetrated deep into my being. It made me gain stature in my own eyes, and I felt my back straighten and my chest become free. She stood beside me, running the fingers of both hands through my hair. Hardly daring to breathe, I held my hands loosely on her hips. I, a starving wolf, could have crushed her with my hunger for tenderness if I had given in to it.

In her gentle voice she said that she would throw the other man out the next day. They hadn't had anything in common for a long time. Not since he and a couple of friends had been drinking and messed up the room terribly before she came home. She said nothing about slugging him in the jaw. When I thought about that, I took her hand and looked at it. A child's hand, but firm and resolute.

I was clumsy and silent and finally she asked me directly while she dug in my forelocks, "Couldn't we . . . you and I . . . instead. . . ."

"I'm out of work," I answered honestly, "I can't pay the rent even once."

"Who do you think's been paying the rent up until now if not me? And you, sober and reliable as you are, you'll soon find a job."

I didn't want to kick the other one out in the dark though I preferred staying there myself, and I said that straight out to her.

"He's not going to be here anyway," she said, and her eyes turned to hard blue porcelain.

She soon softened up again and started saying some ready-made things about believing my eyes more than my words and other things women think have to be said.

"I got out of Långholmen a couple of months ago," I blurted out brusquely before I knew what I was saying.

I felt her fingers go rigid in my hair. Then she sat down beside me and was quiet a long time.

"How about telling me what happened?" she asked quietly at last.

"No, I'd only lie to you; force of habit would make me conjure up some bull. Try to make myself look good. It's just as well I was on my way. Why cram you full of the wickedness I've been mixed up in?"

I got up to leave. The woman and the comfortable room stood

142

there in front of me like barriers to be overcome. Something was compelling me to relinquish them for the bitter night and the wrecked car. They seemed like an ephemeral vision from my dark path. I stopped for a moment, then was driven on.

"You'll come back," the lily shouted, running after me to the door. "I won't ask, I don't care what you've done."

But I left and when I was on the stairs a word engulfed in a sob caught up with me: "Numbskull."

Two cats fighting were making a terrible racket as I walked across the dark yard. Then they took off past me, and the shrieking started again farther away. A little clear window opened, and a round, bare arm shook out a garment. It must have been about nine.

Back at the junkyard on the town's decaying outskirts, I saw that the fence had been fixed during the day. Two new white slats grinned derisively like a pair of fangs at me. When I looked up, I saw two rows of new barbed wire sitting obstinately above the fence around the yard. Between the slats I glanced at my junked car. It glared back with its old lamps as if thinking, "Well, aren't you coming in so I can get some sleep?"

I wandered around the whole night. I had plenty of time to agree with ten or so brothers of misfortune that it was hell to have been born. The conversation was short, on a street corner or a bench. "Got a cigarette?" "How long you been pounding the streets?" "Yes, damn it, it's hell." "Damn it, you ought to. . . ." "The nights are getting cold." "Yes, good-bye, hope things get better."

I met many victims of the unemployment and welfare offices during those days, and with acrid voices they etched out a journal of misery I wish I could lay before the eyes of the well-nourished. I saw big, strong hands withering away from dangling unused; heard the first, dull portent of revolt's drum in a raging boot-kick against a trash bin.

Foreigners who stay at the Grand Hotel[11] and are feted at lun-

11. Stockholm's most exclusive hotel.

cheons at Town Hall make statements about having come to the world's cleanest and richest town. Then the major newspapers print them in delighted boldface type on the front page. Which one of the blusterers has given ear to the symphony of the cat, rat, and welfare alleys? Or has gone there with any intent other than to look at the town's picturesque districts?

I participated in a party that could have meant prison for the man of the house. He had earned an extra five-crown note and had concealed it from the unemployment office. He spent the note on a fear-filled party for his old lady, kids, himself, and me. He wanted to have a man to talk to, he said. To console him, I boasted that if he got caught I would write to the papers about injustice.

When I think back on all I heard and saw, only one word comes to mind: "Goddamn!"

A structured, transparent veil of falseness lies over the whole thing, and those supposedly being helped smother under it. They are helped to grow apathetic, so who can blame them when, after having their cards stamped a thousand times at the agency, they adopt the motto, "I don't give a damn!"

I ran into the lily's man and another fellow as I was lurking about in the vicinity of her alley. They stopped and called me names—he had been kicked out and thought it was my fault. I shouldn't get the idea he was blind and dumb. He had seen my devilry with her well enough. What I needed was a good whipping, he said, and the other agreed with beerish sympathy.

"You, a man who gets punched in the mouth by a little girl!" I responded as any other man would have done. And then I had to throw in that I wouldn't be scared if the alley were full of the likes of them.

They shook their fists at me, called me names, and threatened me. If only they could get me in the right place, damn it! And I didn't think I'd be in on the freight business when his old aunt died, did I? No, not a disloyal louse like me. The fellow standing next to him was a real pal and he'd be the manager of the business.

The real pal looked pleased and mechanically called me names to merit his position.

I left, but slowly, so they wouldn't think I was afraid. The farther I walked, the more they raised their voices. I turned around and saw that a couple of others had joined them. They were having a real go at my treachery with curses and clenched fists.

I won't deny that I would stand staring into the girl's window now that I knew she was alone. I saw her once; she opened the window and lingered there a long time. I wasn't far away from her, but as usual I was too slow on my feet. Just as I was thinking of stepping out and saying "Hello," she mumbled something and slammed the window shut. I felt like I had caught my nose in it, and walked away in disappointment to begin a new night of trudging.

I saw pitch-black water flowing under the bridges during those nights, and many freezing gusts of wind shot out from the street corners, pierced through my clothes, and shook me like an old dog. I walked in a half-daze for hours, a numbing fatigue blunting and obscuring shrill reality. One morning in the street sweepers' gray light, I saw dry leaves whirling and dancing in front of my feet, but when I stopped, they had vanished. I sensed a dark figure in every doorway, but it was gone when I looked for it.

I derived some pleasure from the hallucinations, thinking I might be on the verge of sickness or insanity. (Not raving insanity, just the gifted, mildly muddled kind.) Both fates seemed like salvation.

My disgust for coupon food gradually abated, and I became very careful about the times for my daily feast. I waited as long as possible into the afternoon and stayed in the food joint as long as I could stand the waitress's go-to-hell looks. No tips from coupons, and the table occupied for hours. What could a poor girl do?

All this time, my home stood more clearly in front of me than ever before. Everything took on great and meaningful value, from the chimney sparks on a winter's night to the fly-crowned drop of milk on the bench cover on a midsummer day.

I was down again, so down that the boundary to happiness couldn't be far away. I sensed it now and then, in a fleeting aroma or a fit of shivering. One night I felt tears welling sensuously in my throat, and I walked outside town and experienced an indescribable freedom, light as down. The black ground was so friendly, and the rows of lanterns doubled as they radiated through my tears.

I entrusted myself without reservation to the hand that hit me; I don't know why I looked up, but I did, saying, "You know best; I won't complain."

But if someone had seen me then and accused me of being religious, I would have punched him in the mouth.

The night had been windy and hard to cope with. I had been to the girl's window twice. I had a little stone in my hand and was thinking of throwing it at the window. But nothing came of it; I felt I couldn't accept warmth and protection from a woman when I had nothing to give her in return. I had the country boy's disgust for the nickname a man got who lived on a woman's good will. That the woman had a job and kept to one man at a time made no difference in this case.

I complained through the counter window one day, saying that the welfare money was just too little to live on. I got upset and overheated but didn't gain a thing. Inside the window, the barrier was ready for such pedestrian assaults. A mass of damned well-thought-out phrases lay ready at hand to throw in your face. What could a poor, clumsy mouth on the outside of the window do? Leave with the coupons in his fist and be glad for them.

I left the window, outtalked by justice and convinced that I myself had been unjust in everything, that I should be glad for the crumbs I got, and that society was merciful. I should, as usual, be silent and thankful.

When I heard their skillful talk and saw its effect on me, I thought with terror about how helpless an ordinary human being was before their laws and institutions. Their trained word-manipulators were indifferent to his case; they only wanted it finished by lunchtime.

I, of course, had seen and heard that more lenient legal paragraphs could be found for an upper-class woman than for an old crone on welfare. The hungry bread snatcher was punished just as severely as the car-and-boat-buying embezzler, no matter how white and respectable the judge's beard hung down over the criminal code.

It would probably never be otherwise. The judge sentences his equals for a salary; the lawyer defends, destroys, or is indifferent, all according to the possibility of personal gain. Who thinks of them as human beings, alive and trembling in their rags, when all the finger has to do is glide across dead, unbending, idiotic paragraphs? Written in inflated, incomprehensible language to confuse the victim and gain respect for the terrible comedy.

According to paragraph such and such, clause so and so, the judicial board will now pronounce the just sentence. . . .

Thus I reflected bitterly, sitting on a bench in the empty park. The time for stamping my card would soon be past, but I had been gripped by sloth and swore there was no use even trying.

I refused to go to the food line, thinking vindictively I would as soon starve to death. I didn't think about the fact that no one would care. There was no reason to hold my body and soul together with their damn one-a-day coupon meals.

I saw angry, poorly dressed housewives ladling beef stew and potatoes out of the welfare kettle one day. "Society depends on a happy family life," some important statesman and philosopher has probably said. Those housewives were going to feel so happy when they could have a pile of meat and potatoes to put before their husbands and children.

It wasn't enough that the husband was unemployed; the right

and joy of making food for the family had to be taken from the wife, too. But when the doorbell rings, all you can do is open the door and let in the stern clerk from the unemployment office, who makes sure the man is at home and properly unemployed, at the bottom of the barrel.

A respectable woman with a fur-lined baby buggy looked at me with arrogant curiosity as she walked by, but I didn't give a damn about her.

You're probably some vice president's wife, I thought. The unemployment office has a director too, high above the lines of blue coupons and Högalid[12] stew. I wonder if he had ever been down and seen the bent, gray-bearded men clawing at the pittance on the counter top and counting it with watering eyes. In the twilight of life!

"They're going to do away with the unemployment office and replace it with another, better system," I heard some old men saying as they clinked the beer bottles they were furtively drinking. "Better" would probably be like back home, when the district poorhouse was rechristened a "home for the aged."

Beer, the drink of forgetfulness, runs down the small streets, flushing away what little self-respect remains after you waltz through the many different doors of charity.

Seen from the bottom, a visit to a food joint or a couple of beers seemed like an oasis for the unemployed man wandering in the desert. I saw it and felt it. The noise from the beer hall can sound like the music of the spheres. I heard it. Old careworn faces turned more sociable from the bitter brew and momentarily exposed their miserable teeth to existence.

A flock of schoolchildren walked past my bench, swinging their satchels and books.

"Children," I thought, watching them. "Beget children," comes the injunction from the tall buildings, "beget children down there!" The coupons rustle and the stew flows cursedly through the cat- and rat-infested alleys. The stamping lines can be longer still! Onward in the spirit of defense and the sewing circle! Create more

12. Högalid is an area in Södermalm.

148

children to be caught in the death-spider's web: barbed wire! Make sure the children have elbows to push with and flat feet to stand on in line. They'll be needing them.

Because I didn't get my card stamped one day that week, my welfare money was cut off, and it would be three more weeks before I got it back again. A life of trudging started up again, but I felt more apathetic now. My external concerns meant less and less, but I clung fast to the trees, the sky, and the philosophical thoughts I had from my books.

I had hallucinations occasionally and they still heartened me. A cloud transformed itself above Essingen,[13] becoming a huge face looking at me with sleepy cordiality and something like soft eternal peace across it. One night when I was dozing on a bench at Riddar Canal,[14] someone called my name in a loud resounding voice. I opened my eyes and saw the water glittering before me. A night trolley rumbled across the bridge; the bells of the road barriers clanged at the tunnel. I felt safe and sat up again.

Out of my own darkness, a hundred or a thousand years old, emerged a vision. I was standing by a big forest. The landscape was open on the other side with mist and haze beyond it. Then, miles and miles away at the horizon, a huge army of horsemen came riding, their weapons glowing through the mist that occasionally enveloped them. They didn't move along the ground; they moved high in the mist. The horses whinnied as if they were right next to me.

One time I was bodiless, running with the shadows of the clouds across the fields on a stormy and sunny day. My joy and relief were boundless.

Because my eyes and ears weren't what they used to be, I could hardly believe it was Father coming toward me on a street near Klara Church late one morning. Of course, I recognized the brown

13. Island west of Långholmen and Södermalm.
14. Canal near Riddarholmen, which, together with Gamla Stan (Old Town), comprises the oldest part of Stockholm.

eyes, the gray moustache, and the satchel with the dangling straps; I'd taken it to town, too, several times. I looked myself over quickly—well, I wasn't so bad off that I couldn't be mistaken for a fairly well-dressed laborer.

If I had been able to, I probably would have slinked off into a side street, but Father had already seen me. His face glowed with happiness and surprise as if he couldn't really believe what he saw.

I softened up my facial features as much as I could, though I think all I came up with was a foxlike grin. We shook hands, and Father said it was damned good luck to run into each other just as he had stepped off the train.

"I've been wanting to get hold of you," he said, and his look darkened. "Someone back home said I should ask at the census bureau. We thought that maybe you had written, but the letter got lost."

"I never got one off," I answered. "I've had so much to think about. Odd jobs here and there."

"The tablets didn't work out then—I thought so. Well, it doesn't matter. You have to come home with me anyway. Mama . . . your mother . . . well, she's pretty bad."

Father told me more while perfume-smelling office girls bustled in every direction. Mother's condition had grown worse just after I left, and now she hardly had the strength to be up and around. You shouldn't think the worst, of course, but it had to be cancer. I knew it was in the family; it had taken her parents. How about a bottle of beer?

"Your mama," Father said at the cafe table, "has had a lump in her stomach for several years. But it hasn't caused her any pain. Now it hurts and she's getting thin. What do you think?"

"Didn't you have it checked?"

"You know how she is; I haven't been able to get her away from home. But you'll come with me, won't you? She's made a fuss about that night and day. I couldn't do anything else but come looking for you. We've had damned good luck running into each other."

Father emptied his beer glass and wiped his moustache in satisfaction with his right hand.

"Is she in a lot of pain?" I asked.

"Who knows? She doesn't say anything when she's sick. It probably hurts and will get worse. Let's each have another bottle of beer."

And as if Father sensed my economic woe, he added, "It'll be nice to treat my son to a bottle of beer here in town."

I sat thinking that I couldn't go home with Father with things the way they were now and looking the way I did. I wanted to go home like a man, paying for my own trip, wearing decent clothes, even if I had to steal to do it.

The whole time I envisioned Mother's face with her pursed lips and large, anxious eyes. Anxious for me, for Father, for the cat and the chickens, but never for herself.

And so I started talking. I convinced Father I couldn't get away for a couple of days, and finally he accepted it. I had some business I had to finish, I said, and exaggerated quite a bit there at the beer table. Father might have thought that all Stockholm would go to hell without me, the way I carried on.

Everything went well; Father left that afternoon after having bought what he wanted to take back in the flimsy satchel. I didn't break my chattering and lying facade a single time. He went home to Mother with good news—I would come the day after to-morrow, as soon as I finished up my business. That didn't sound so bad.

Night came back, without any hallucinations but filled with a single aching thought: how could I get home again like a man? I asked the alleys in Gamla Stan,[15] the black water of Strömmen,[16] and Skinnarviksbergen Park;[17] I walked for five hours with my eyes glued to the pavement to find a wallet or watch. After midnight I

15. "Old Town," the oldest part of Stockholm, surviving from the Middle Ages.
16. Strömmen is the area of water between Gamla Stan and the Royal Palace and the island of Skeppsholmen to the west.
17. Skinnarviksbergen Park is in the northeast part of Södermalm.

found an unopened envelope on Strandvägen,[18] and my heart started suffocating me with its pounding as I tore the envelope open. I stood staring like an idiot at the contents for a long time before I realized what it was. It was a rubber, a nubby gag condom shaped like a rooster's head complete with comb. I hung it with a disappointed grin on the door handle of a distinguished house.

Around lunchtime the next day, I bit the head off my tattered haughtiness and walked up to see a minister. First, I looked in a telephone booth and found a minister's name in the book. I picked one but took another one along too just in case.

I was admitted without having to give a particular errand, and I felt a little better at once. A girl invited me to sit down in an easy chair and wait, but after she left I took an ordinary chair instead. The big chair made me uneasy with its engulfing comfort.

There was an upper-class smell in the room, and that always made me feel morosely uncertain. What I most wanted to do was leave, but I knew that when I got down to the street again I would berate myself for my cowardice. I sat there, having continuously to wipe the sweat off my hands. A clock struck eleven ringing chimes somewhere in the apartment.

The minister who came in was a middle-aged man about my size. He had an ordinary face and a pair of calm eyes. I probably would have liked him if I hadn't had to ask him for help.

He greeted me pleasantly and directly, one man to another, without being unctuous in bearing or behavior. He sat down by his desk and looked for a moment at a picture of two children.

"You wanted to talk to me?" he said.

I had thought about explaining my recent difficulties as an introduction but couldn't. How could I think a stranger would be interested in that? He had his own problems—those children he was looking at were probably his, so he had a wife and home. That was plenty for him to worry about without some devil off the street throwing himself on top of him with more shit.

18. Strandvägen is a famous street on the strand of north Stockholm. It faces south toward Skeppsholmen.

Besides, my voice turned hard and lifeless whenever I was going to talk about myself. Like the coffee grinder at home when Mother stood by the stove grinding.

"I've been in Långholmen," I said finally, staring sternly at the minister. I both hoped and feared that he would throw me out.

He didn't fall off his chair, though he probably was surprised.

"Yes, well," he said after a moment. "You're not the only one . . . I mean . . . well, I can understand. . . ."

Ministers, Salvation Army soldiers, and other religious types usually point to God with one hand and anxiously pinch their money pouch closed with the other when someone asks them for help, I thought. If this one here did that, I'd show him.

I didn't have a very clear idea of what I would show him, but the notion had crossed my mind that it would be hard to get in touch with some God in such a rich and comfortable room. I would tell him that to show off my poverty. I would say that Jesus had walked barefoot and chewed on wheat, that His life was more like mine than the minister's. The only times I could sense God as I conceived of Him were when I was in need or in the rain or wind.

But that was only a streak of light; it flashed through my darkness and was gone. The radiance of the person in authority dominated the room, and all I could do was mobilize the army of my misery against it. Again I found myself out of breath in the middle of scraping to the bottom of the last year's hell, and I didn't blame it on anyone but myself. Not by calculation—who could calculate, when I felt myself following so far behind my words?

I met the minister's eyes twice while I sat there, and it was very strange. He said nothing, but he got up once and walked a few steps across the floor before he sat down again.

The whole matter didn't take very long. I had soon reached Father's trip to town and Mother's cancer and just then, at the most important part, my throat thickened and fell silent. In a kind of rage I stood up and walked to the door. I didn't give a damn then about whether the minister helped me or not.

Outside the door was a hallway, and the girl who had let me in was there doing something. Rigid and blind with tears, I saw her surprised eyes focused on me. I also saw a glove that had fallen on the floor, and smelled the aroma of upper-class food.

I was all the way down the stairs when I heard the minister come out after me. He called something, but the words echoed in the stairway and I couldn't make them out.

I walked up and down a few streets before my head cleared enough for me to overlook my debut as a beggar. I had promised my father I would be home the following day at the latest. How could I manage it? Only by walking again, the way I did when I got out of prison. It would be different now, with long dark nights and muddy roads, but that didn't bother me. Arriving home was the hard part.

I took the country roads this time, stealing apples and carrots to live on. Everywhere people were picking potatoes in the fields, and the smell of potato tops uprooted big clumps of my childhood from me. Yellow, thin, autumn hawkweeds still thrived on the ditch banks, and stinking chamomiles had taken over the fallow fields.

At dusk the second day, the ragged conqueror, Lars Hård, came out of the woods near the church. I wasn't afraid of walking past the poorhouse standing right next to the road; the old people with their dull eyes wouldn't be able to see who was hurrying by in the dark.

I saw the alms board by the road and tried to remember what was on it. I hadn't read it since I was in school.

> *You are wealthy, fat, and hale,*
> *I impoverished, thin, and pale;*
> *Many friends the rich man knows;*
> *The poor man has not one of those. . . .*

So went the poem on the old board. There was an iron box with huge fittings on it under the board and a slot to put your alms in. The key was in the rectory.

My thoughts flew back to my childhood and dragged out a

memory. We each had a two-öre piece, a friend and I, and we were about ten years old. It was a lot of money for *statare* kids, who would normally get a five-öre coin apiece for Christmas. I had found my two-öre piece outside the church door, and my friend had fooled his parents into thinking he had to buy a new slate pencil. In school, we had two-öre slate pencils wrapped round with colored paper.

Some strange catechism angel had whispered in our ears to offer our riches to the pitiful old folks in the poorhouse. We strode self-importantly along the hill with the two-öre pieces in our mitts, ready to do the good deed. We stepped onto the stone platform, and a hoarse croaking made us look up toward the poorhouse. An old witch on crutches stood on the stairs, shaking a bony yellow fist at us.

"What kind of tricks are you up to?" she hissed. "Get away from here!"

We ran away with the rescued two-öre coins. We bought two large twists of red-striped candies instead.

I counted on coming home after dark. A train came in about that time, so I could easily have been on it. In the lamplight of the hut it wouldn't be so clear how my suit looked, and I could probably fix it up a little the next day unnoticed.

I saw our pale red bedroom window between the bushes that had grown a little sparser. There were already dry leaves on the road, and sometimes the wind came, inviting them up into a murmuring, whispering dance in the dark. Behind me, I heard the big forest's eternal roar rising and falling.

He was no fool, that Jesus, I thought where I stood. He spoke for all ages. Here stood another prodigal son sniffing toward the house of his father after coming straight from society's pigpen. The difference between the son in the Bible and me was that I wasn't the swineherd but one of the swine instead. Mother Sweden, her skirts updrawn, had poured the swill down from above for me and a few thousand others to gobble up thankfully. The slaughter would probably follow, too, in its own good time.

The comparison seemed flawed, but I couldn't come up with anything better right then.

It was time. I was so used to sneaking around that I had to make myself plant my feet squarely on the ground. I tiptoed to the steps, but when I reached them, I stomped decisively. I had come on the train, goddamn it, and had had trouble getting away from my job.

Coughing and making a racket, I went in. Father was sitting by the table, which was set for three. They had counted on my coming as I'd promised.

Mother came out of the bedroom, and I saw at once that something was completely different about her. She was thinner than before, but her skin was clearer. Her half-blind eyes looked as if they watched something standing far away by a clear horizon waving for her to come. As if she were unsure about whether she should go or stay with her family. Father's brown eyes asked me with heavy melancholy, "Well, wasn't I right?"

We sat down at the table and I, rugged and thick-skinned, was able to put some life in my parents. I saw them loosen up and felt the calm float up under the ridges of the roof. They didn't say a word about the time I had been away, and I occasionally and uneasily asked myself if they sensed how it had been for me. On entering the hut, I had said that I hadn't had time to buy anything to bring home with me.

"So what?" said Father. "We have what we need anyway. There aren't any kids here to buy candies for. It's just as well. That way you didn't have to lug something here from the station."

There was no question about my leaving again; Mother couldn't be alone while Father was at work. Something inside me blossomed when I felt that I really had a place, that I was needed. Mother didn't have the strength to be up for very long periods, but from the sofa her eyes followed all of my actions as best they could, and her gentle, weary voice guided me among the pots and pans.

Sometimes she sat outside in the sun by the cabin wall, and I wondered if she knew that she would never again get to see the days grow longer and a new summer arrive. That the September sun lighting up the dew was the last that would warm her withered cheeks.

I heard voices outside, and when I looked out through the window, I saw a two-toothed old bitch from the estate talking to Mother.

"We'll just see how long they'll let him be loose now," said the old bat, poison dripping from her voice. With her witch's face and tawdry rags, she looked like a strange and terrible plant among our asters and sunflowers.

Mother looked timidly at me when she came in, but I acted as if I hadn't heard anything.

When she slept, I walked into the woods and visited my old haunts again. I went to the cave and figured out exactly where the upper-class girl had lain that time I dragged her in there. The glade where the little blonde girl looked at me with teary-eyed affection as I ripped at her clothes. Where was she now and who had her radiant blue love, I wondered, waxing as lyrical as a stableboy.

We'd had a rock, too, which was privy to a great deal, but now it stood there, sullen and cold as night. I sat on it and looked down in the grass. The ground was autumn-still; only one or two insects walked on stiffening legs toward death in the frosty night.

The autumnal sky above the tops of the spruce trees—emptied of larks, of warm summer gusts of wind, and washed clean of the God and angels of the catechism—was bottomlessly deep and blue.

White clouds came driving rapidly and playfully forward from the West. For a while they covered the whole heaven. I sat waiting. As soon as an open well of blue sky appeared, my soul's long snout was in it.

Not because this is a novel but because it's true, there was a girl standing in our kitchen one day when I walked in. She was standing there and I didn't know her. Mother said her name was Eva and that she had helped her with everything before I had come home. She was the daughter of a family that had moved in a few months earlier.

I looked at the girl but harbored no hopes. I knew well enough that she had heard my story. Well, I didn't give a damn; she could think what she wanted.

She was no Courths-Mahler[19] beauty and wasn't very well dressed either. She looked up quickly at me, and I saw a couple of wise little shy eyes. No bitchiness or contempt for Långholmen in them.

It was as if Mother wanted to have the girl out of my presence; she said several times that since Lars had come home she didn't need any more outside help. Besides, she was better. We could get along by ourselves.

The girl looked back from the doorway, and our eyes met with a kind of cold interest.

Every time Father came home, he walked straight in to Mother; he bent his head under the doorframe, and his boots clomped dully on the rag-rug floor.

"I've sent for the doctor," he said one day. "You'll probably be able to get some medicine that will help you on your feet again."

"As long as it's not too expensive," Mother sighed from the sofa.

She lay quietly most of the time, following me with her eyes as I was cleaning. I wished sometimes I could show her more spontaneous tenderness, but I was hindered by a feeling close to shame. It came from my school days and the silly poem in the primer about a mother's love until death. It stands immutable through all fates, I thought, and the memory brought with it the agony of those school days, the hard bread and herring, the threats of the cane, and the oppression of the catechism.

I don't believe Mother was thinking about all I had been guilty of, all the sleepless nights I had caused her, all the jeers from the neighbors. Her thoughts probably didn't go far beyond the corners of the hut. When she was in pain, she would turn toward the wall and pretend to sleep, but I saw well enough the painful contortions of her body.

19. Hedwig Courths-Mahler (1867–1950), German authoress who wrote some 200 novels of almost no literary worth. Many of the novels were translated into Swedish.

"Does it hurt, Mama?" I asked, but she didn't answer, breathing harder, instead, as if asleep.

The clock on the wall ticked slowly. It was afternoon, and an apple-tree branch hung outside the window, looking in. It was the clear time of the asters; some leaves broke loose with a soft snap and floated to the ground.

The doctor didn't spend much time with Mother, and when he left, I followed him out with his bag. Outside, he said that it was very advanced cancer, inoperable.

"You can take her to the hospital, if you want," he said, looking out over the reddish-yellow garden.

"If she wants me to," I answered, "but not otherwise. How much longer does she have?"

"Just a few months. It'll be harder to take care of her later on."

The doctor nodded and backed his car out through the gate. Yellow leaves clung to the tires.

"We should pick some lingonberries before the frost gets them all," Mother said, looking out the window. "This is the first autumn I haven't had the strength to be out picking them."

We talked about it and decided I would go out and pick berries after lunch once Father had left. I thought to myself that I'd ask the girl Eva to look in on Mother once while I was gone. I had run into her a couple of times and had exchanged a few words with her.

"She's gone to the woods," her mother said. "She took a basket and left. Is it you, Lars Hård?"

"Yes."

The old woman wiped her hands on a rag and stared at me in surprise. Well, I did look like a normal human being after all, dressed in work clothes and everything.

I walked on, thinking that maybe I would run into the girl among the lingonberries. Mother would probably be all right alone for a few hours. The sun was shining on the rag rugs in the room as I walked away from home; it was warm and quiet. Lying on her back, Mother told me with closed eyes where the basket was hanging in the attic.

The forest was full of brown, wet mushrooms that looked like cow droppings. It smelled of bog myrtle and frozen marsh plants. The sedge had brown spots on it, and a falcon hung on quivering wings above the swampy land. The lingonberry tufts were a half-meter high among the dwarfed pines.

I didn't look purposely for the girl, but kept my eyes open all the same. After about an hour I caught sight of her; she stood leaning against a big rock instead of picking lingonberries. The forest opened out, sinking in one direction, and the treetops lay like a sea down below. In the distance you could see a village on the horizon; it looked like a mirage set deep in the neighboring district. The girl stood absolutely still, staring out over the expanses of land. The basket sat on the rock beside her.

I came up from behind, my footsteps silent in the moss. I set my basket down and sneaked carefully forward, one step at a time. Then I grabbed her by the shoulders and spun her around.

She wasn't the kind who screamed to the high heavens, but she gasped and turned a little white. I saw the terror in her eyes turn to recognition and then a tiny touch of happiness. We kept standing like that awhile before I let go of her shoulders.

Then we stayed close to each other picking berries, and our eyes met occasionally, lingering and a little shy. I saw the supple lines of her body when she bent over, and I wished that I could have such a woman, not just for the moment, but night and day, a woman both intense and affectionate. A creature with soft breasts and arms, hot breath, and red cheeks. Well, the cheeks didn't have to be so red; the main thing was that they were hers.

She wasn't afraid to sit next to me a little later, and I realized it had been three years since a girl had been so close to me. She had a hole in her stocking, and if her clothes smelled a bit of the crofter's kitchen, I wouldn't have had it any other way. In any case, having a girl sitting next to me in the forest made it seem like a holiday. The moss glared green in the sun; everything was totally quiet. A little gray bird flew from one dwarfed pine to the other, pecking in the bark for larvae. There was a slow rasping from its claws as it climbed the trunks.

Nowadays a man can't sit next to a girl without touching her. I didn't want anything in particular; I was happy just to sit there with her close to me, but I started to touch her because I didn't dare not to. When I caressed the wisps of hair around her ears, she smiled, but when I put my hand on her leg, she took it and placed it gently but firmly on the moss.

I knew that the morals of most country girls follow chronological principles. Nothing can happen the first, the second, or even the third time. There had to be a steady relationship first.

But I also knew that many of them even while resisting start breathing more heavily, closing their eyes, and relaxing. I continued trying to touch her but at the same time was afraid she'd give in to me. Who knows after three years of hunger whether or not you forget how to eat? It would have been too awful to botch it.

I grabbed for her and pretended to be eager and experienced in the area but hoped she'd get away from me. She allowed me her head and arms but successfully defended her legs.

For a long time I had heard short, crisp shouts in the forest. They sounded like a moose, but moose were rare in the district. We talked about it but couldn't figure out what it was. "Aaa-ooo," it echoed, and immediately afterwards, "Aaaoo."

Anxiety suddenly rose in my chest when I heard the shouts. There was something of life's misfortune in them, something that once again had pursued and caught me. The threat of society, the threat of the laws that seized and shook my innermost vital nerve echoed through the forest.

"It's coming closer," the girl said, and we both forgot I was holding her calf. By then I realized it was coming for me and bowed submissively before my fate.

"Aaaars Ååååård" it resounded now on this side of the hill.

"What in Jesus' name!" the girl said, and I felt her leg go rigid in my hand.

I got up and walked toward the shout without a word. It wasn't long before it rang out among the sapling pines a hundred steps from me: "Laaars Hååård!"

"Over here!"

"Over there? Then why the hell didn't you answer sooner. I've been running around yelling my head off!"

A red panting face beneath a state cap came out of the bushes.

"Follow me back to the road," the county deputy said. "The sheriff's sitting there waiting in his car."

"I see."

I didn't ask him anything; I just started walking beside the servant of the law. I had time to catch a glimpse of the girl; she stood watching in terror by a rust-red birch bush that had got lost in the pine forest. She had probably heard that the sheriff was waiting on the road. Her mouth hung half-open and one of her stockings was pulled down a little because of my inability to let things alone.

"Nice autumn weather," the county deputy said with gruff compassion.

"Yes."

"And a hell of a lot of lingonberries this year."

"Yes."

"I was blowing the chaff off the wheat when I heard a car stop outside, ha, ha, ha. It was the sheriff. I had to go in, put on my cap, and leave, that's all there was to it. Ha, ha."

God, I thought with reeling despair, they've been around asking Mother about me. Two men in uniform, the county deputy and the sheriff, had walked into her bedroom and asked about me with self-important voices. I wonder . . . and I half-ran with the state's breathless stableboy by my side. I soon saw the shiny car on the road.

"Are you Lars Johan Hård?" the sheriff asked, indifferent.

"Yes."

He took out some papers and shuffled through them. "You bought some clothes on credit and despite repeated reminders haven't lived up to the obligations of your contract. Here's the paper from the city debt collector concerning the repossession of the goods. You still have them, don't you?"

"Yes."

"Climb in and we'll go get them. Was it just fifteen crowns you owed?"

162

"Yes."

"It's been three years since you bought it. Haven't you been able to pay that little bit?" the sheriff asked and started the car without caring about any answer from me.

About a hundred meters from our hut, I saw something grayish-white among the flowers in the window. I knew what it was. We stopped by the gate, and all three of us saw death itself, with Mother's face, looking through the window. It was among the fuschia and geraniums. Something like a grin of terror on it had stiffened in expectation. The eyes were an empty black under the high forehead, white with anxiety.

"Hm," said the sheriff, "Deputy, you can go in with him and fetch the suit. Give Lars Hård a receipt for it."

I ran in and the county deputy came coughing after me. Mother turned toward us, the strange, rigid expression still on her face. She held on to the window frame.

"It's nothing, Mama," I said quickly, "they're not taking me in; I'll be staying home. It's just some silly little thing."

I took her and led her into the bedroom. She wheezed and hung heavily on me. I laid her on the sofa and found the old suit that had accompanied me from clarity to clarity, from hard labor to prison. Pressed and cleaned at Långholmen by the murderer, Gyllenpalm, they had told me on my release. It was through and through a judicial suit.

"Did two uniformed men have to come out after this rag?" I said to the county deputy. "Did you think I was going to defend it to the last thread?"

"You just do what the sheriff says," the county deputy answered, coughing behind his fist for my mother's sake. I wrapped the ragged suit in some paper for him.

"So there we are; now you can just as well go back to the woods again as far as we're concerned and pick lingonberries," the deputy said encouragingly, playing equals with the sheriff.

"Huuiii," Mother wheezed in the bedroom.

The engine rumbled and the car backed out through the gate. Yellow leaves clung to the tires as they rolled round and around.

Mother lay with her eyes closed, and I saw the fear gradually leaving her face. She had heard the sheriff's car humming away without me; I was still walking about, at home, in the room. She heard me build a fire in the stove and wash potatoes for when Father came home. Soon his bootsteps would sound on the floor and all would be well.

"What was it about this time?" Father asked, and I knew that the estate was already buzzing merrily and breathlessly about the sheriff's visit to the Hårds.

"Nothing—they just took that old suit I owed a couple of crowns on."

"Oh, that—forget it. We'll find a way to get clothes."

"You can't understand what it's like," I said, feeling a childlike desire to whimper. "You can't understand what it means to have all the bastards after you."

"Oh, I understand well enough," Father answered. "It takes a while—and then it passes, and you'll see what it was good for. Don't give in, even if the devil himself pulls up in a car one day."

And Father clomped heavily in to Mother in the bedroom.

In the dusk when Father sat reading aloud to Mother from the district newspaper, I walked to the woods to fetch the basket. Right at the edge of the forest there was a figure sitting on a stump.

"I brought your basket," she said in embarrassment as she got up. "Here."

"You're sitting there catching cold," I said, and my heart lit up because she used the familiar form of "you" with me.

"I didn't have this many lingonberries when . . . I left," I said. "You put berries in my basket."

"Oh, no."

"Oh, yes."

We laughed and I held her hand all the way home. It was cold and rough on the inside from work, but I wouldn't have had it any other way.

After a while, Mother could hardly stand without help, and then it was a good thing my hands had turned soft during the last few years of upper-class living. If I was out and Father had to lift her, she complained bitterly about his rough hands when I came back.

She grew anxious the minute I was out of sight and nagged jealously when I came home. I didn't tell her I was seeing the girl, but every time I did, I saw that Mother knew it. Her eyes, which mostly looked far off in the distance, would take on a wily, mistrustful expression.

"What do you do out there so long?" she asked. "I had to get up. You shouldn't pay any attention to the neighbors."

And if the girl came in and asked how she was, she answered sullenly or not at all.

She didn't have anything bad to say about the girl; it was probably just that she didn't want to share the affection of her loved ones those last days. The warmth and power streaming toward her from her two big rugged men she needed for herself.

I saw the minister approaching the hut on the yellow path, and I felt ill at ease. He was a good minister, no question about that. He always began with the body when he wanted to reach the soul, and that's a good strategy among the meek and the poor.

I had nothing against the minister, but I was afraid he would talk with Mother about religion and such things, fulfilling his duty as warder of souls. Then she would guess she was about to die. Although everything was darkness for her now, she had her lucid moments when she could see a long way.

I was standing in the doorway as the minister approached. He had a white beard and a pair of good eyes.

"Good day, Lars," he said. "I've heard your mother's sick."

"Yes. . . ."

"I would very much like to have a few words with her. She isn't unconscious, is she?"

"No, but all she needs is to be left in peace. It's not a good idea to disturb her."

And I didn't get out of the way.

"Are you going to keep me from doing my duty?" the old man asked meekly.

"She doesn't need anything," I mumbled, letting him through. I walked in before him and touched Mother's shoulder.

"The vicar was just walking by and heard you were sick, Mama," I said to her. And I saw with relief that there was a haze in front of her eyes. She looked without anxiety on the representative of the next life.

I was on tenterhooks while he talked about a couple of cases like Mama's; I shuddered, fearing he would say "cancer." But then he took a book out of his pocket and leafed through it.

"May I read a little for Mother Hård?" he asked.

Mother didn't answer, and the vicar shot a glance at me.

"The vicar wonders if he should read for you, Mama," I translated, but she didn't answer me either.

Then he read something about the Apostles. I heard the names Luke and John. What good does that do, I thought. Here a person spends her whole life, slaving for her loved ones, and when she's worn out and about to die, another old human being comes along and reads something about a couple of old fishermen who lived and died two thousand years ago.

And I thought further: if he could just say what the flickering light was farthest inside a human being that drives him to pray to the universe in need and solitude. For many years he had led a group of reading, hymn-screaming, and sighing human beings in an old stone building from the Middle Ages, but the real question was whether a single sound ever forced its way out of the stony grave.

When the minister closed the book again, he looked at me and said that even if I despised God's Word now, there might come a day when everything would be different. Then I would seek it with humility in my heart. At first I thought of answering, saying I knew his big, happy humility better than he did, but then something told me that inside him, too, there was another human being.

Maybe he lit up with gold in there. But he had to tend to his position, play his role to the last breath—like me and everyone else. He had to live his own life.

And when I looked at his friendly eyes and white beard, I felt a peaceful blue flower bloom inside me. For the first time in three years, I freely offered my hand to a stranger and he took it. He said a few words about my taking good care of my mother and about how industrious and self-sacrificing she had been. When he took Mother by the hand, she came to her senses a little and searched inside, though she said nothing.

I watched the minister go. Yellow leaves rained down on him under the aspen trees in the enclosed pasture. Despite the cloudy day, the leaves glowed as if sunlit.

You have Luke and John, I the spruce and the aspen, I thought as he left. Who knows whether or not we can light our paths with such different lanterns.

The herring barrels stood in a room at the back of the general store. I asked for two kilograms of herring, and the fat, religious store owner opened a door and said audibly to someone in the office, "Listen, keep an eye on this one out here while I go back to the storeroom."

I felt the old rage well up in my chest and rush into my muscles; in a moment I wouldn't know what I was doing. I felt my legs coil for a leap and my eyes haze over.

Just then, a man came into the store carrying a large carton with no lid. A large wreath of asters was sticking up out of the carton with broad last-respects ribbons glowing white on it. I stared at the wreath, and a mass of feelings muddled my anger and guided it to the open graves down by the church.

The storekeeper's poison arrow didn't work in me for long. What does it matter what someone says, I thought, following Father's old recipe. In fifty years both his jaws and mine will have rotted, but the trees will still be standing as they are now. Don't pay any attention to the fat, mean devil.

And when he wrapped the dripping, staring herrings in an old copy of *Fädernesland*,[20] I looked at his shallow, bleary eyes and the brush under his nose.

You aren't any happier than I am, despite my hard life, I thought. I wouldn't exchange a week with you even if I got your business and house into the bargain.

The lackey clerk peering out from the office disappeared. The store smelled of herring, snuff, and pettiness. At home it was clean, simple, and strong.

I was unhappy all the way home. It was a dazzling Indian summer day, and the crofter in the pasture had let his cow out in the garden patch to eat up the tops of the rutabaga. The cow shone red and white in the distance.

The runestone was standing in the rocky clearing, telling mysteriously of the Viking who had gone away with Ingvar to the East over a thousand years ago. I compared the Viking with the shopkeeper I had just left and wondered to what extent man might have improved in a thousand years. I compared myself with the Viking too but found no points of contact. At least I admired and understood him. The storekeeper lived only for money and slimy gossip about people in the district.

I laid the package in the grass below the runestone and traced the runes with my finger. I saw the spirit of Eirik, who had carved the runes on a clear late autumn day more than a thousand years ago. At the request of the Viking's wife Inggerd, as it said.

Then there were no factories and unions, missions or churches. The few human beings who existed were strong and simple, without all the rottenness that spread its smell everywhere now. Damn it, just think of the men lucky enough to live then instead of today! They must have been much closer to God, or whatever you want to call the essential things, than we are, they without noise and wars.

Wars—yes, they existed then too, but what a difference if you

20. *Fädernesland* is a Swedish scandal sheet that ceased publication in 1927.

think about a handful of warriors on the ground who bled to death singing in the green grass compared to a modern division, which dangles screeching in barbed wire or is eaten away by poison gas in a grenade hole.

These were my thoughts as I plodded home with my package. In the autumn mud of the pasture path, I saw several tracks of old ladies' shoes, broad and bearing the weight of a hundred kilograms. One had walked so bow-legged that you might think by the tracks that two had been walking abreast.

The tracks headed up toward our hut, and I thought—what in the hell? Didn't the old ladies from the estate know that Mother's time for coffee klatches was over if it had ever existed at all? That she was battling her hopeless battle against a creeping disease on her bedroom sofa? And that the terrible son in the house had come home? He who had kept their nerves tingling during the past three years?

With these thoughts in my head, I pushed on, making the mud on the path smack. A shapeless anxiety had grabbed me by the hair and dragged me forward, and I regretted I hadn't hurried.

I saw nothing unusual outside. Leaves lay so thick on the path through the garden that I couldn't see if the tracks passed through them. I had hung the hut key where it was visible on the doorpost, but now it was in the door.

There was nothing unusual in the kitchen, but I heard strange noises from the bedroom. A solemnly sniffling mission-house voice. I was through the kitchen in three bounds, running into the bedroom door so that it flew open. I saw three pious women by Mother's bed. One of them was on her knees raising a pair of veined, bony, clasped hands toward the ceiling. The other two held their clasped hands on their fat stomachs. All three had red or green cardigans on, and to my bitter gaze, they seemed like three splendid specimens from Satan's mushroom patch.

Mother lay twisted toward them with something unnatural in her position. Her eyes were directed with rigid wonder and dawning terror at the one on bent knees. She had probably wakened after the three women had taken their positions, and now her poor brain could understand nothing more than their horrid prayers, which they offered with simultaneously importunate, ingratiating, and fanatical voices.

The first woman merely stared at me when I threw her out in the kitchen, her cardigan fluttering. The second screamed and scolded, but she went too. Then I walked toward the kneeling one, and she stretched out her clutched hands toward me, screaming in a shrill voice to God to forgive the terrible sinner for Jesus' sake.

She was thin and dry, and when I snatched her up from the floor and shoved her into the kitchen, she flew as if she were already an angel. Then I went out after them, and they backed toward the door shouting shrilly. I found out I was a murderer who wouldn't let his mother go to the hospital, that I should never have been let out of Långholmen, and that I would soon be back, they would see to that.

"Poor, poor friend," said the fanatical thin woman in an indescribable tone, wildly happy because I would burn in the fire and brimstone lake while she howled praises and ripped on eternity's harp with her bony claws.

But I didn't let them get away with it. I piled it on them with a big shovel. What else could I have said but "Go to hell, you damn old bitches!"—which ninety-eight percent of all Swedish men would have said in my place. After chasing them outside, I settled down, but they kept turning around and railing at me all the way through the grove. The leaves floated peacefully down over them like over the minister a couple of days before. The leaves had no sense of discrimination; they settled as easily on the shoulder of an old woman's green cardigan as on a minister's black coat.

I didn't know then and don't know now whether Mother was aware of her cancer. She never complained and didn't ask me what the doctor had said. She remained silent, looking death stubbornly in the eye as he approached her bed.

After the three women and their angry clamor had disappeared behind the grove, I returned to her. The haze had left her eyes.

I thought about what the three holy women had called me and

asked Mother if she wanted to go to the hospital. She said no, strongly and full of anguish. "Not unless you find it hard to have me home and want to get rid of me, Father and you," she said, and then I did as Peter did.[21] Feeling I was needed and the best one to take care of her was like a gentle hand caressing my heart.

Soon Mother didn't let me go for even half an hour. During the evenings when Father was home, I sneaked off to exchange a few words with the girl, who always came out when I walked by. Mother nagged after me constantly, twisting on the sofa.

"Let the boy be out for a while," Father said. "You don't need to worry about him; he can take care of himself. Go to sleep, or should I read the serial story for you instead?"

I came into the bedroom one evening, happy from a timid kiss I had just got. Mother was sitting upright on her sofa, looking around in distress with uncomprehending eyes. Father was sitting beside her.

"He may have been in some accident," Mother said.

"Who?" I asked.

"Lars, of course," Mother answered irritably.

"I'm right here."

"Good heavens, are you home?" Mother asked, satisfied, and lay down again.

"You should stay at home with her as much as you can," Father said in the kitchen. "It won't be long now. The death owl hooted in the oak tree when I was at the woodshed a little while ago."

Then some calm days came, and we started hoping Mother would get well again. She sat at the kitchen table with us and could walk by herself. But one afternoon when I came in after being out for a while, I found her lying on the floor. She had twisted herself where she lay, and those large, dark eyes were looking toward the door when I came in.

"Is it you?" she asked. "I tripped on the rug, and now I can't get up."

21. See Matt. 26.75. After denying Christ three times, Peter "went out and wept bitterly."

From that day on, she didn't move from the sofa except when I carried her. She lay looking toward the apple-tree branch that swayed in the wind or hung motionless, seeming to peer through the window.

"The grass had grown tall around the hut when you were born," she said once clearly and out of the blue.

I tried to give her as good care as she'd have received in a hospital; I washed her morning and evening and combed her long brown hair. I broke the seat out of an old round chair and made a pretty good toilet out of it.

When she slept, I quietly cleaned the room. I carried out and shook the rag rugs, dusted off the royal family,[22] and polished the bulging pewter tankard on the side board. The clock creaked, tired from thirty years' use, and Mother breathed so softly that I would walk up gripped by fear and put my ear to her mouth. The old furniture in the bedroom emitted a heavy afternoon melancholy. I knew it so painfully well, every stain on it, and the auctions they had been bought in, most of them before I was born.

I had to defend my mother once more against do-gooders. A couple of community leaders came to say she should be moved to the home for the aged, where she could get better care. The woman manager there was knowledgeable about caring for the sick.

"No, she's staying here," I answered. "She doesn't want anything else."

"Don't pay any attention to what a sick person says. We'll have them come and fetch her in the morning."

"No, you won't. I'll throw any bastard out who tries to take her. I'll use that if I have to," and I glanced at the axe standing by the stove in the kitchen.

The parish gentlemen were above arguing with me, but they said on their way out that they couldn't be responsible if things remained as they were.

22. It was very popular at the time to have a picture of the royal family in the home. Pictures were available from mail-order firms.

"A scoundrel like that should be put away for good," one of them said, stepping over a mudhole in the path.

"Yes, he can be deadly," the other answered. The leaves fell silently on them too.

A couple of days later they came back again with the doctor. He asked me a few questions and examined Mother as fast as he could.

"It's probably best for her to go to the home for the aged and get better care, Doctor," said one of the men ingratiatingly.

"She doesn't want to," I said dubiously. "She'd be uncomfortable there. Father and I won't go along with it."

The doctor thought and looked around the room. "She seems to be in good hands here," he said. "She's clean and has fresh air in the room. In any case, there'll be a change soon. Let things stand as they are."

And he nodded cordially to me as he walked away in the company of the two crestfallen bigwigs.

Then no one else came to see us except the neighbor girl. She was shy and poorly dressed, but I, Lars Hård, who was almost thirty years old, saw a glow cover her from her long eyelashes to her worn-out shoes. Mother no longer realized when she was in the kitchen with me. She would come and say a little timidly, "I'm going to the store and thought you might need something."

And when I held her, she looked down and picked at my coat sleeve or played with one of my buttons.

I soon knew that Mother's cancer had reached her kidneys. Several times a day I had to change the sheets under her, and while I did so I sat her in the chair Father got when he turned fifty. The upholstered sofa—her joy—was completely ruined, but she didn't realize it.

"The sofa," Father said in the kitchen, "what does that matter? The damned old thing! We'll just throw it out . . . afterwards."

And he looked out the window to conceal the grief in his brown eyes.

Long lamplit evenings filled with Mother's rapid breathing and the rustling of Father's newspaper. The cat slept on the bed. Sometimes it walked by Mother's sofa and sniffed but didn't jump up.

"A cat'll never jump up next to someone about to die," Father said to me in a low voice.

The cat lay sprawled on the bed now. While Mother was up and around, it could never jump up to lie on the bedspread and had to stay in the kitchen.

One evening as we sat together, an owl started hooting right outside in the apple tree. Father lowered his newspaper and looked meaningfully at me, and Mother twisted on the sofa without opening her eyes. I ran out in a fury, grabbed a white-painted stone by the flower bed, and sent the stone flying at the owl so that the leaves and branches hailed down. I thought I saw it fly off in the darkness.

One day when I was going to change Mother, I discovered a decimeter-long, terrible gash in a fold in her stomach. Only with the greatest difficulty could my quivering hands do what they had to do. Mother was conscious and asked for Father. She didn't know about the wound.

I didn't tell Father what I had seen, but I telephoned the doctor.

"I understand," he said, "but now the worst pain is over. She'll start to pass away in the next few days."

She had never complained or said she was in pain. And I always thought women complained about the smallest matters!

Throughout those final days she appeared to have turned toward something else. She would become lucid occasionally and ask something completely unexpected about some little thing in a drawer or something that had happened a long time ago. Between times, she seemed completely absorbed in some other kind of seeing and hearing. She would press her lips together from the pain, gathering her soul beneath her high forehead for the journey from a body that had already begun to disintegrate. But only I knew that.

I had the feeling that her every step away from life became a step into something else and that she was surprised in her trance. I had seen surprise and astonishment on the faces of many dying people. Seeing Mother walk toward death, I became even more convinced that unbelievable things exist beyond our knowledge no matter how powerful a pair of spectacles or how long a beard knowledge may wear. Things that can't be seen through a telescope but come through the universe like a wavering clear melody and set everything akin to them in sensual vibration. The loftiest things always come as gifts and elude all cheap, saucy explanations.

And although I was alone and pungent as the wormwood that I saw yesterday by the rock in the field wet from the rain, there were moments when I felt great compassion for everyone who had things well-ordered and comfortable. The scoundrel Lars Hård was burning with a happiness that rose up from the earth, passed through him and up into the universe.

Then I knew, without being religious, that Mother was facing no danger where she lay. She was in good hands—exactly whose didn't concern me. I had only to believe. She didn't need anything; I didn't need anything. Everything would work itself out.

"I'm going to scrub the kitchen floor for you," the girl Eva said. "You can't get down on the floor yourself, a big fellow like you."

And she laughed through white teeth, giving me a hasty, shy look as she tucked up her skirt.

I sat watching her as she scrubbed; I heard the brush's familiar scrubbing sound against the boards and smelled the fresh aroma of soap. Then I went in to Mother, but she was far away and didn't answer me. When I saw her from the door, the bony parts of her face protruded so sharply that my nose caught a slight scent of the grave. I walked quickly out of the bedroom.

In my anguish for Mother, I sat down to watch the girl scrub. I could see her legs up to the knees, soft and supple, swinging rhythmically under the updrawn skirt. Her waist was slender and her arms beautifully soft. I wondered where she had come from. Her parents looked like a couple of gray, rough gateposts.

I started to feel a gnawing hunger for her, and I think that the feeling tugged with a thousand fine threads in her. Her face had taken on a little color, and I thought I spied a hint of happy anxiety in her eye whenever she looked up at me.

After she had finished scrubbing, we sat on the sofa. The striped rag rugs stretched themselves out, three abreast, smelling of fresh wood; the stove burned briskly. The coffee pot was on. Outside, the aspen trees stood straight and still, almost leafless. They had spread an inch-deep carpet of light yellow leaves over their feet.

The girl was sitting beside me. She hadn't let her skirt back down. Her slip lay thin and black over her legs, a touch of white glowing through it. We didn't say much, but everything was different from in the forest—tremblingly ready and unavoidable. There was fire in her skin and in my hands. She sank backward and opened up like the crown of a flower. Her face was more beautiful than I had ever seen it before; her eyes closed in fine lines, and her lips moved softly and only to answer mine. I envied her gift for staying away so long. The stove was burning and crackling.

I heard a sound from the bedroom and slipped quickly, silently away from her. She raised her hands weakly for me but let them fall back again. She didn't open her eyes.

While life was moving softly and warmly in the kitchen, death was sitting in the bedroom by Mother's bed chattering its teeth. Mother had opened her large eyes and was staring straight across the room with a strange expression. She breathed more calmly than before. I huddled down in front of her, trying to meet her eyes, but they passed light gray straight through me into an endless distance.

That look scared me and I ran out into the kitchen again. The girl lay there as before, and when she heard me return she put her arms around my neck with her eyes still closed and drew me down toward her face.

"Dearest," I said for the first time in my life, "Run for Father, will you? Don't scare him. Don't race all the way up to him. Just tell him to come as fast as he can."

She came to life, leaped up, turned my head away, and breathlessly straightened her clothes. Her eyes were still tender with terror. She didn't ask anything, just ran off like a dot of sunlight among the aspen trees.

Mother's gaze was still fixed at the same distance when I came back into the bedroom. I talked to her in anguish, damning myself inside for my hard voice that fit in so poorly just now. I searched for her pulse and finally felt a weak beat or two.

Soon I heard hurrying, thunderous steps outside. Father came in and tried to set his boots on the rug silently and close the door without a sound. Without a word, he walked over to Mother and tried to look into her eyes as I had just done.

"Should we send for someone?" I asked in a whisper.

"No," Father said, "who would we get? She lay picking at the bedspread this morning. I knew then the end was near."

The girl was sitting out in the kitchen—my girl. When I came in, she got up as if I were a dignified person.

"I'm back," she whispered timidly, "I thought you might need someone to run. . . ."

We sat with Mother for hours, Father and I. Finally she relinquished her gaze, which was looking out into nothing. It was better then, and we started whispering busily. Maybe she would live a little longer yet. People had known cases that were almost miracles.

When the fire in the stove died down, we heard the girl build it up as quietly as she could. I walked out in the kitchen and put a little food out on the table. I whispered to the girl that we would eat a little cold food, but she could make coffee for us afterward.

I took control, began making decisions. I went in to Father and asked him to go out and eat a little. I would sit by Mother in the meantime.

It was a gray, clear dusk and the apple-tree branch peered curiously in through the window. In the corners and under the bed it was already dark. Mother breathed very irregularly.

When I looked out in the kitchen, I saw Father's forceful bearded head outlined against the window. It was bowed forward, but he wasn't eating. On the plate were a piece of bread and two potatoes he had peeled. The evening light was brighter in the kitchen, and I could see tears falling from Father's eyes, rolling down his beard onto the table. The cat sat at his feet, looking up longingly.

After the girl had gone, we both sat with Mother again. I was afraid it would be hard for her at the end. I had read about the death struggle, and though I had sat by many deathbeds, I had never seen anyone actually fight death. I imagined the horse of death as a black horse coming and standing by the bed, ready to carry the soul away on its back when it was over. The soul, I thought, looked like a rider of the mist.

I tried to get used to the idea that Mother would die soon, but I couldn't fully grasp it. She will die and be buried; you'll never see her again, I said to myself, but it didn't go any deeper than that. A mist kept me from seeing to the bottom.

The person lying there is Mother, I said to myself. It's like looking at a skeleton. It once carried and bore you into the world. You probably remember the big, splendid woman she once was. You'll die, too, in a few years—it's not so far away; a few years are the same as an instant. The girl Eva will lie looking like that some day as well.

"You think she can hear us now?" Father asked in a muffled bass.

"No, she's probably far away."

"I think so too. No, you can't keep the thoughts from coming and going at a time like this."

"What are you thinking about, Papa?"

"I was thinking about my father. He escaped from Russia and came here, became a soldier, married a minister's servant, and then I came along. Their hut, with its little garden and lice-infested furniture, was their main concern while they were alive. When I was twenty-five, I got married to your mother here. We bought a little junk at an auction, and then you came along."

"Yes, a lot of good that did."

"You don't know that yet. Oh, you'll probably get married to the girl who was just here, and then you'll have kids. You'll line a few cheap things around the walls, you too, and live in them.

178

There's our cupboard, there's our table, you'll say, but there are millions of cupboards and tables in the world. . . ."

"Well, so what?"

"I don't know, but I think there should be something more. Something standing behind everything the whole time, explaining why it is just so with only little differences. My father, you and I will have lived identical lives, so one would have been enough."

"Identical, you say."

"Mostly, yes. If you get married, you'll become a *statare*. Did you think I wanted to become one before I met your mother? Like hell!"

"I don't know, Father," I answered, "but maybe you can't see the whole road until you get high enough. Grandfather may have seen a rain shower glittering above the Russian steppes and that memory has stuck a little in you and me. You usually talk yourself about the yellow bedstraw outside your soldier's hut, and so it sings inside me and will inside my children too maybe, if I have any. So we blend together into something; we don't have to know what. Whether we become *statare* or not is less important."

"Yes," Father said, and now we noticed that there were longer pauses between Mother's breaths. I talked to her, asked her if she recognized me, and suddenly she responded with a noise. She said something indistinct in someone else's voice. I got up shivering. Things had become so alien in the room. Terrified, I looked over at Father, but he just sat there, silent, black-bearded and unreal.

Suddenly I got scared. Mother and Father. . . . What is this? The room seemed a fantastic image that had tumbled out of some alien surrounding. I felt sweat breaking out over my whole body, but I soon got over it, and again I could see all the years and the things around me through normal everyday eyes. I felt myself latching on to the present, and still trembling, I took Mother's wrist. Her pulse was weak and uneven. It was seven o'clock.

The clock struck nine. Father's heavy head was hanging down and his eyes fell closed. Then he gave a jerk and looked at me in embarrassment.

"I'm used to going to bed at eight," he said.

"Lie down on the sofa in the kitchen, Father," I said. "I'll let you know if anything happens. We have to go on living after all," I added practically.

By ten, Mother's face had undergone a strange change, and I knew it was preparing itself for its return to the earth. It had the color of earth, and her breathing was no longer regular. From the kitchen I could hear Father turning on the sofa; he probably couldn't sleep.

The feeling of unreality came back as the clock struck ten; a mass of images moved without logical connection inside of me. Mother's face in the weak lamplight, the window's black holes, the brown door to the kitchen turning hallucinatory again, and dreams ripping themselves loose from their surroundings. I watched everything tensely as if from a corner. But it didn't last long.

"What now?" I asked myself, taking control again. "This is not the right time, I'm sorry—there are more important things afoot. Mother is dying, after all."

In the end, I forgot about myself because of Mother. I felt enraged at my impotence. I couldn't fight the creature sitting silently in the room, waiting, but I knew him well enough by the tingling in my spine.

There must be someone who can get the best of him, I thought. Praying? Oh, damn it!

But the thought circled around again and came back. You know, of course, that there's great happiness beyond adversity and death, something inside me said. Do you think it's reserved for you alone, you idiot?

I felt for a moment like a child whose Mother was going far away. I clutched my hands together and let my soul move far into the universe. There I said right out into the silence and emptiness: "I hope you'll pardon my butting in like this, but she is my mother, you know. If anything can be done for her, may I ask you to do it? She's worked and slaved and she'll be there any minute now. I don't know what it's like there, but she deserves your consideration. . . . Amen."

I seemed to hear a noise from the back door, but my thoughts were far away by then. Maybe it was Father walking out. But when I looked up, I met Eva's eyes in the door before I had time to unclasp my hands. I was ashamed and lost my temper.

"What are you staring at?" I hissed, and she disappeared into the kitchen.

Mother drew a deep quivering breath. The next one did not come for a painfully long time. The moment I went out into the kitchen, Father got up from the sofa.

"I haven't been able to sleep," he said. "Eva's come. Is she suffering?"

"I think so."

Father went into the bedroom. The girl stood silently in a corner.

"Oh dearest, forgive me," she said when I walked over to her.

"Sh! Be quiet. Why are you here so late?"

"I saw a light on and thought I might be of some help. I couldn't sleep."

"You can stay here in the kitchen if you want to," I said, and I was glad to see her even though Mother was dying in the bedroom.

When I went in again, I had the feeling that the silent visitor had moved up to Mother's pillow. The tense expression was gone from her face; the painful swallowings had stopped. Her chest rose softly a couple of times.

Then it stopped. . . . We got up. No, it rose once more; she made a scarcely noticeable movement to get comfortable, then lay still.

It's not any easier for men, even though they don't give in to snuffling and crying. The silence just after Mother's death was of an indescribably special kind, and I was glad in a way that there were only two gruff men present.

Then the ordinary things had to be done, and my need to be fussing around returned. I tied a scarf, a brand-new one, around Mother's head to hold her mouth shut. I positioned her for the rigor mortis that would soon set in. Father looked on through dismal eyes, and I saw that he, like me, still couldn't comprehend that Mother was dead.

"We'll both sleep in the kitchen tonight and open the window here for Mother," I decided. Father clomped heavily out into the kitchen and pulled off his boots.

I walked through the garden with the girl, and though Mother was dead my heart felt rich. The lamplight tumbled out the window onto the red and green leaves, which hung absolutely still in the night. Beyond, the great forest was roaring though the night was completely calm.

The kitchen was empty when I came back, but peering into the bedroom, I saw Father standing bowed over Mother and heard him saying something to her. I pulled my head back before he could see me. It already felt cold in the bedroom.

I don't know if Father slept that night, but I don't think so. We both snorted once in a while to fool each other. After midnight, anguish gripped me—the thought that Mother wasn't dead; I had heard about suspended animation. And it was so cold in the bedroom now. What if. . . . But I had heard her stop breathing and felt that she was almost cold. But maybe I should have held a mirror in front of her mouth before I took it for granted. What if. . . .

Maybe Father was lying there with the same thoughts; in any case he lifted his head and watched me as I walked into the bedroom. The cold air struck me. I had hung a rag over the lamp, and in the darkness Mother's face with the scarf around it seemed just as it had when I left her.

Suspended animation wouldn't look that way. I stood there for a while, looking at her. The draft from the window played with some strands of hair by her temple, the same strands I had seen the summer wind moving once when I was little. Mother and Father had been sitting on the ditch bank with a picnic basket between them. Mother was buxom and splendid, and I remember Father playing with the strands of hair and laughing through his black beard. A long, long time ago.

We put Mother in the woodshed, and I chopped long, straight junipers that would stand watch around her. The old crones came running to us and were helpful, as usual, once someone had died. They forgot who I was. They called me "Lars" and consulted me as if I was a normal, decent human being.

182

I walked to the cabins beyond the hard-frozen roads so I could hire pallbearers for Mother, and I didn't care that they were still staring curiously at me after those three years. Their faces were glued to the window panes when I came up, and they responded sullenly to my greeting.

"Oh, we'll do it all right," the crofters responded to my request.

Almost all the crofters had black suits, but there weren't many *statare* men who had anything to change into for holidays and formal occasions. Father's suit was thirty-five years old; he had married Mother in it, and in it he would follow her coffin.

It was a clear November Sunday when the black carriage with the silver-bronze fixtures came to fetch Mother. She had never traveled in such splendor before. A pale red sun was shining on the birch trees' frozen bark, and the driver clapped his hands together while he waited.

The black crowd following the hearse wasn't very big. About twenty older people in old green coats or 1880 cardigans with puffy sleeves. The pallbearers had on their derbies; they came down off the dusty beams of the attic every other year or so.

The deacon stood ready, and when the hearse swung round the bend, he started his solitary chiming in the tower. From the gate where we stopped, I saw the rust-yellow dirt piled by Mother's open grave. On one side the planks stuck up in an uneven row. There were magpies chattering in the elm trees by the stone wall.

The crofters looked like ravens as they buzzed around the hearse, threading the black bands under the coffin to carry it into the church. One poor old crofter must have borrowed his derby; it was plainly too big for him. When they started off with the coffin, it slid down his forehead, blocking his vision. He jerked his head back, trying to force it up again. When I saw his moustache wiggling, I knew he was swearing to himself about the hat.

We *statare* were allowed to sit at the front in the gentlemen's pews that Sunday. Gentlemen observe a certain courtesy toward death even when it visits the *statare* hut. If the patron bares his head for a *statare*, that's how it will be when he's lying in his own coffin.

Or maybe it isn't for the *statare* after all but for the black-clad visitor who comes even to the palace.

Once again I saw the angels from my childhood hanging there with their trumpets. They were fat-cheeked and heavenly as always. The same red cloth lay on the altar, garishly informing one and all about its donor, a rich old widow, dead for thirty years. That's what's called doing a good deed in secret.

The atmosphere of punishment and perdition hung thick under the vault, left behind by hundreds of generations who quaked in their pews because of the blustering avenger above the clouds. The monk's religion of terror—"I am the Lord, your God, a powerful avenger"—was a doctrine for the days of birch bark bread.[23] A eunuch's dream!

The minister started speaking. I didn't hear much of what he said. I never did ask about it, but I knew it had something to do with the Sermon on the Mount. I paid attention a while when he talked about the mountain as mountain.

"Maybe it wasn't a high mountain," he said, "and maybe there was grass on its ledges. It may have been peaceful with a gentle voice trilling along the slopes to each and every person. . . ."

I liked that. But in the notes from the ancient organ there was too much of the grave, sin and retribution, darkness and death. Palm trees and harp music. The old women in the pews howled out their pitiful rendition of the hymn, but the old men stared with deadly silence into the hymnbooks.

I tried to show some manners at Mother's funeral, to be as devout as the others. But when the minister picked up the little spade, I was back at it again.

Human cowardice and the ineradicable sense of comedy come together here, I thought. Christ, a man who died two thousand years ago, has as his task to dig up from the earth countless millions of human beings during what is called the Last Judgment.

23. A reference to periods of poverty and famine in Sweden when ground-up birch bark was mixed with flour as an economy measure.

Provided, that is, that as children they had a few drops of water poured on their heads while a magic formula was chanted.

But to make sure the other countless millions will be left lying there or maybe called to everlasting hellfire, people say jealously, "It isn't the water alone. . . ."

No, surely not.

There's nothing better than the church for shutting off contact with God. Let the kingdom of the dead, the avenger, and the sacrament all molder down there in the souls' grave. They can't stand sunlight and clean air.

Such were my thoughts though I was sitting in church at my mother's funeral. I must be the freak people take me for, a monster of hardness and sin. But then how could I be happy deep inside?

Next, the crofters carried Mother out. The borrowed derby slipped down again, leaving its wearer flat-headed. He didn't swear this time, but he certainly would later. "Goddamn hat," he would probably say when he got home.

As the black cover with the aster flowers on it wobbled down under the earth, the women began their traditional sniffling. Behind their handkerchiefs, they trained their evil eyes on me to see how I would act at my mother's funeral. See if my hard, sinful heart would melt. But I frowned down into the open grave and met the asters' terrible stare. "Oh, no, you don't," I thought. "Lars Hård doesn't cry on demand."

But when we walked silently toward the gate—Father and I— I thought I heard Mother screaming aloud for us from her grave. Unknown powers grabbed my shoulders, wanting to wrench me back, but I kept going. Marching rigidly homeward, we didn't dare talk or look at each other, Father and I. The old crones and old men followed after; they had wine and coffee to claim for their walk-on parts. Their November Sunday had been made a little more enjoyable because of Mother's death.

The girl Eva took care of the guests for us, and from the corners came the heavy-handed joke—"Oh, yes, she could very easily replace the old woman now. It's not so easy for two men to live

185

alone, ha, ha, ha. But Lars, the restless bird, would probably fly away soon, ha, ha, ha."

The next morning I walked out to the grave. The sun shone on the frozen flowers. There was peace and beauty in my heart; I had nothing to fear. Anything at all could happen to me; Mother wouldn't walk restlessly around the house, anxiety for me lodged in her dark eyes and behind her tight lips.

In the afternoon I walked into the woods to take stock of my assets. Yes, I would keep on living, watching the days come and go; that was enough in itself. I would be of some use to Father in his solitude, and I had the girl who looked at me with shy, warm affection.

Although it was November, the sun was warm, and a stiff rustling came from the bottom of the ditch as the frostbitten rushes rubbed against each other. There was a little pang in my heart when I thought that Mother didn't exist any more, that nothing had changed because she was gone.

It was all the repulsive things I had been through that made it possible for me to go on living. The sum of all evil was good. Whatever I had might be taken away from me. Maybe I would be driven out into the mud and hell yet one more time, but my reserves could only grow from now on. I imagined I was clambering up the side of a mountain with more and more lying behind me as I looked back.

Nothing noteworthy would ever become of me, but that didn't bother me any more. I would remain here in solitude and not stick my sensitive nose into the crowd again if I could help it.

In any case, here I sat, Lars Hård—the son of crime, prison, and anxiety—and my heart was rich with an unconditional happiness. It had sprouted like a wildflower out of the garbage heap of misery inside me, and an unfamiliar sun far in the distance was shining down on it.